A Taste of Liberty
Task Force 125, Book #2

Lisa Pietsch

Table of Contents

Copyright

Published by Defiance Press & Publishing, LLC

Bulk orders of this book may be obtained by contacting Defiance Press & Publishing, LLC. www.defiancepress.com.

Defiance Press & Publishing, LLC

281-581-9300

info@defiancepress.com

Task Force 125 Series

One

Sarah blinked back the sweat that rolled from her forehead and into her eyes. Her hair fell from her ponytail in long locks sticky with perspiration and clung to her cheeks. Her breath was hard and fast as she dodged hits and blocked kicks just to keep up with the man she was fighting.

My God! He's a machine.

He had about thirty pounds on her but he was wiry and fast. He was throwing everything he had into the mix. He started with Muay Thai boxing, but, when he did a Capoeira flip and spun his body in mid air from a standing position, a chill raced up her spine. She'd never seen anyone as fast as this guy. She threw punches at his face, shoulders and stomach and never made contact. He'd dodge, twist, spin and jump just barely avoiding her hits and kicks. His years of training and experience in hand-to-hand combat were obvious.

Focus, Sarah. Focus.

The midday sun in the Nevada desert beat down with a steady blast of 102 degrees. Each breath was like taking a drag off a bonfire. The heat, dehydration and near exhaustion wore her down, and Sarah slid into a reactive, defensive mode where her movements were automatic. She knew she couldn't win this way but the bright sun lulled her into not caring.

Her opponent flashed a wicked smile. His eyes sparkled like the trillions of grains of sand glinting around them. The relentless sun and heat slowed her down and he made the most of it. "Come on, sugarlips. Is that all you got?"

He spun to his left.

The pain of a powerful blow to her right shoulder woke her from her daze, and her adrenaline surged.

Son of a bitch!

His teeth glistened as he grinned. "Papa's gonna take you to school."

Her jaw tensed. "Not today, Papa." Sarah saw her opening for a kick and took it. She put all of her weight behind a roundhouse kick aimed for his neck and a clothesline takedown but the soft sand beneath her feet shifted and she slipped, kicking him in the head instead.

They both fell.

Sarah scrambled to stand quickly. As she did, she turned to see the man still lying on the ground, unconscious. She dropped to her knees beside him. A chill raced up her spine despite the heat. "Jason? Jason " She placed two fingers on his neck.

Good heartbeat. Damn. I'm gonna need some help with this sandbag.

This wasn't the first time one of them had been knocked out when they were sparring. It was becoming all too common as Sarah's fighting skills advanced. She walked over to her Jeep and pulled her phone out of the door pocket. She pressed the number *One* and then the *Send* button.

I hope he answers.

Two

Vince poured himself a cup of coffee from the room service cart. The suite at the Hotel Timothy in Transnistria was passable, but the coffee was just plain great.

Will looked out the window as he lit a cigar. "Man, this country has a smell all its own."

Vince sat on the small sofa. "Yeah, it stinks of evil. It's the only place in the world where you can buy anything, from AK-47s to Zambian children. I just want to get this deal set up and get home."

Will looked up from the empty street market carts below and squinted at Vince through the cigar smoke. "In the years we've been doing this, I've never heard you call Las Vegas home before."

"I guess it never really felt like home before."

Vince's phone rang. He picked it up off the nightstand and smiled as he noticed the caller ID. "Hey, you."

Sarah's voice came in clear despite the continents between them. "Hi! You in town?"

I wish.

"Nah. East of the Volga."

"Too bad."

The left side of Vince's mouth curled into a half smile. "Why? Whatcha got in mind?"

There are a few things I'd love to do with you right now.

"Well, I got a little trouble here."

Vince sat upright and his mind switched from horn dog to military mode.

"What is it? Are you okay?"

"Yeah, I'm fine. It's Jason. He's unconscious."

Vince sighed, relieved that Sarah wasn't in trouble. Jason was always unconscious for one reason or another. Booze, bar fights…he lived hard. He could take care of himself. "Not surprising for a Saturday but a little early, isn't it?"

"No, we weren't drinking. We were sparring about a mile southeast of the gypsum mill. I slipped in the middle of a roundhouse kick. I think I hit him in the temple."

Vince didn't like the idea of one of his men unconscious out in the middle of the Nevada desert. "Jesus, Sarah! Why don't you guys use the ring at the Camp?"

"Well, hell, Vince. We've been working out in the ring all week. Besides, the shit doesn't go down in a ring. We needed some elements of reality."

"Yeah, yeah. I know, but they have a medic there. I can't have you two beating the shit out of each other out in the middle of nowhere."

"It's not like we weren't prepared. I've got him in the shade and a bottle of water standing by. I'm watching him now."

"If he doesn't come to in a couple minutes, call Brian."

Sarah chuckled. "Oh! There he is. Sleeping Beauty awakes."

"You're a lucky girl. Now go get the medic to check him out."

"Will do, boss." Her voice softened, betraying the personal feelings she always tried to keep at a professional distance. "Come back soon."

Vince's face softened. "Bye, babe." Vince sat back and took a long breath. He loved hearing her voice.

Will interrupted his thoughts when he spoke. "Vince, this is just between you and me, man. It doesn't go any further. What are you gonna do about Sarah?"

"Nah, she's alright. She and Jason were sparring, and she knocked him out for a minute. Shit happens when you train hard. You know that."

Will shook his head. "That's not what I mean, man."

"What are you talking about then?"

Will took a thoughtful draw on his cigar. "We're never gonna find another agent like her. She's got the whole package—looks, brains and pretty frigging handy with a knife. You know, after our last mission, when the Navy found Hassan's body, his chest was cut wide open. She didn't mess around.

She cut straight through the bone and sliced his heart in two. Anybody else would have just got the hell off that boat and let the bomb do the rest, but she took the kill and then dragged you off the boat with her."

Vince remembered coming to, Sarah holding his head above water as debris from the decimated yacht fell all around them.

I still don't know how she managed to throw me off the boat in time.

"The Air Force don't teach that, man. That's either a hardened operative or, well, a woman in love. Either way, you don't want to fuck things up with her. We want her thinking clearly and on our side when the shit goes down."

Vince rubbed his chin. He just shaved but everything about Transnistria made him feel dirty. Igor Smirnov's dirty little hole in the wall, jammed between Moldova and Ukraine, was the only place he could arrange for such a big shipment of AK-47s, fast and without question. His cover as an arms dealer was beginning to wear on him. He'd seen so much filth and death he wondered whether he'd ever be able to escape it all and just live a normal life.

What is a normal life anyway?

There were times when he just let himself think about what it might be like to chuck it all and leave the CIA's Special Activities Division.

Just disappear with a good woman. A woman like Sarah.

"Hey, Vince." Will waved at him across the hotel room. "Wake up man.

I'm serious. What are you gonna do about the girl? There's no denying there is something between you two. Hell, even Jason picked up on it, and while he's a killing machine and a hellacious bodyguard, we all know he ain't too bright when it comes to the ladies." Will puffed on his cigar and waited for Vince to answer.

Vince lit a cigarette. He knew what was on his old friend's mind, and Will was right to ask about it. Vince had done this work for the C.I.A. for far too long. He was becoming weary of the drug dealers, gun dealers and slavers.

The line between the good guys and bad guys was blurring, and Vince didn't like the side he was standing on most of the time. He had more to think about than just himself, though. Retiring would skew the whole team dynamic. It would take months to work a new guy into the team. Sarah was a fluke. She was only supposed to be the honey pot and gather information. She might as well have been a bug planted by the bed.

As it happened, she turned out to be far better than that and had fit in with the team in no time at all.

Who knew she and I would hit it off like we did?

Vince had to hand it to her though, for somebody they'd recruited out of the Air Force, she was totally professional when it came to espionage. She never broke rank, and she respected the cardinal rule— *you don't shit where you eat.*

Vince refilled his coffee from the room service cart and took a long drag on his cigarette before stubbing it out in the ashtray. Will was right. They needed Sarah for the mission, but he needed her too. He'd tried but he just couldn't get her out of his mind. He walked to the window at the far end of the suite, watching as couples and groups of friends made their way to the nightclub next door.

I can think of better things to do on a summer night than wait for an arms dealer in a shabby hotel in Moldova.

The mission had to come first and there was still too much to be done if they were going to put the hurt on Al Qaeda. Sure, knocking out AQ's main moneyman, Hassan, in their last mission put a crimp in Osama's business, but they needed to get rid of his weapons suppliers and more of his financial network before anybody started thinking about retirement.

"Look, Will, my brother is still in Baghdad, and this is the only way I can cover his six. We've got to get Osama on the ropes and we aren't gonna do it with one or two missions. We've got to be in this for the long haul. All of us. Gettin' all domestic isn't in the cards. Sarah and I are just two agents working together, and that's as far as it can go." He turned toward Will and tensed his jaw. "I've got it under control."

"Alright, man. You know I just need to know where your head is at.'

"It's in the game, Will. It's cool."

The knock on the door reminded Vince he hadn't fully prepared for the meeting. He set his coffee cup on the nightstand and pulled his Sig Sauer pistol out of the drawer. He turned away from the door to buffer the sound as he checked the chamber and magazine. He tucked the handgun into the waistband of his worn Levi's and pulled on a white tee shirt as Will walked to the door. Their eyes met and they nodded to each other. They'd been playing gunrunners for years and had the drill down.

Will opened the door. "Nikolai!" He smiled and made a sweeping gesture with his cigar hand. "Come on in. How about a cigar?"

Nikolai assumed the room. His presence was distinctly larger than his six foot three, tightly muscled frame. It was no surprise to Vince that he was a successful businessman. Nikolai carried himself as if he owned the world. To be honest, he did own a rather large chunk of it, at least in Pridnestrovie. He was speaking on a cell phone, quickly followed by a stern-faced, large, blond Russian who looked like he would have been right at home in the KGB. "Da, da. I'm visiting with some friends, but I'll be on a plane shortly. Don't worry. I'll be there."

Nikolai snapped his phone shut and slipped it into the breast pocket of his black leather jacket in one smooth move before reaching out to shake Will's hand. His long dark hair fell down to his shoulders. He looked like he hadn't seen a razor in about a week, but he carried himself like he was God's gift to the world. He walked toward Vince, strong and confident, and grasped his hand. He gave a wry smile loaded with brilliant white teeth and shook his head. "Mothers."

An Oxford educated Russian with barely a trace of an accent who could write his own ticket and here he is running guns.

"We all have 'em, Nikolai. Have a seat." Vince gestured to the worn but passable sofa and sat as Nikolai did.

Nikolai pointed to the door and scowled at the big, blond bodyguard.

"Andrei, close the door." Nikolai smiled at Vince. "I do not mean to rush you but, as you've heard, I have another appointment, and I cannot be late."

Will remained standing and casually leaned against the window frame, all the while keeping his gun hand free. Vince had Nikolai covered but Andrei was Will's target. If the deal went sour, Will had to take down the bodyguard.

"That's fine." Vince smiled. "We have quite a bit of traveling to do as well so a short meeting won't offend us at all."

Nikolai's bearded face became very serious and his dark gaze grew darker. "There is a problem with your order, my friend."

Gun runners don't generally like to hear that phrase, but it was exactly what Vince and Will were looking for this time. Vince picked up his pack of cigarettes from the coffee table and tapped a Marlboro out of the box. He lit it while offering the box to Nikolai. The slight distraction might keep Nikolai from seeing the satisfaction in Vince's eyes.

Tell me what I want to hear.

Nikolai took one and accepted the lighter Vince offered.

Vince leaned back and crossed his right ankle over his left knee. "What kind of problem, Nikolai?"

"The guns and ammo won't be a problem." He handed Vince the lighter and took a drag off his cigarette. "It is the helicopter that will be difficult."

"I thought I made it clear we had a limited window of opportunity or that part of the deal."

"Yes, of course. That is why I would like to refer you to an associate of mine. He will not be available to meet with you until next month, but he can deliver within twenty-four hours."

Vince stood up and paced a few steps, feigning agitation. It was all part of the plan. He shook his head and spoke almost in a low growl. "I don't like associates, Nikolai. How do I know you aren't setting me up?"

Nikolai ran a hand through his hair and smiled. "Vince, you and I have made a great deal of money together, and I look forward to us doing many years of business together. This is no average associate. I would never disrespect you by referring you to some shopkeeper. Certainly you have heard of Victor?"

Will stood straight and Vince turned quickly toward Nikolai. The sudden movement must have spooked Nikolai's bodyguard because he drew his gun on Will immediately.

Will was just as fast and had a .38 pointed at the man's big blond head.

"Check yourself, man! What kind of pups are you using for bodyguards these days, Nikolai? Call off your dog!"

Nikolai grew stern and his eyes grew dark. "Andrei. Outside. Now." He leaned back on the sofa and took a drag off his cigarette. "I'm very sorry, my friends. Please, forgive the boy. He is too nervous for this job. Perhaps he'll be better suited to cleaning toilets."

"Nothing to forgive. No harm done." Vince assured him. "So, Victor? Really?"

"Yes, of course. He is the only man I know who can produce and deliver what you're asking for."

"Well, in that case, when can he meet us?"

"He will meet only with you. He'll be at the International Arms Expo in Genoa, Italy, next month. I've taken the liberty of giving him your phone number. His secretary will contact you with the details."

Vince extended a hand to Nikolai. "In that case, thank you, Nikolai. I trust the guns and ammo will be delivered immediately as per our agreement?"

Nikolai stood. "Yes, they are on their way to your warehouse in Dubai as we speak."

"*Spaceba*." Vince thanked him in Russian and walked him to the door.

"Please tell Victor I'll be in Italy for the expo as well and looking forward to hearing from him."

Vince closed the door softly behind Nikolai, checked the area for bugs, and looked over at Will who was checking for bugs in the area where Nikolai sat.

"All clear." Will stated.

Relief washed over Vince. "That's it, man! We got a meeting with Victor!

Let's go home and get the team packed up for Italy."

"I'm all for that. I'll call the pilot. You call ops. Let's get the hell out of this shithole, man!"

Three

Sarah's lean, tan body cut swiftly through the crystal blue water of the pool. It was six-o-clock in the morning, the sun had just come up and she was swimming laps at the pool at the Las Vegas MGM Grand Signature where she'd recently purchased a luxury condo, her first real home. She swam laps for an hour every morning around this time so she could have the pool to herself.

Signature condos were owned by high rollers and otherwise nocturnal types.

Nobody there woke up before noon if they could help it.

The monotonous, rhythmic strokes of her swimming allowed her mind to wander as the cool water washed over her, lap after lap. She wondered when she'd see Vince again. She hadn't seen him since just after the team's boat trip on Lake Mead when they returned from the Mediterranean a couple months ago. Her mind kept going back to that day before the mission when she was in Vince's cabin. He'd thrown her down on the bed and kissed her like he meant it. After that kiss, there was an unspoken promise of more to come when they'd finished the mission.

Then, after their mission debrief, Vince disappeared without a word.

Maybe that was just how the team did things, but Sarah expected something more, something personal instead of professional. She knew she shouldn't but there was just something so right between the two of them that she couldn't help herself. Maybe he couldn't deal with the fact that she'd slept with a terrorist to get information. Maybe the fact that she saved Vince's life twice was just too embarrassing for a Marine. Hell, maybe he was just trying to let her down easy by going away for a while.

Maybe it's for the best.

Reality struck when Sarah hit her head on the edge of the pool.

Jackass.

She stood up to see if anyone had witnessed her moment of oblivious stupidity and breathed a sigh as she confirmed she was alone. She dove back in and continued her laps. Not a day went by since Sarah's stay at "the Camp"—the C.I.A. training camp where she'd recreated herself and accepted a job as a spy with the agency's Special Activities Division—

when she didn't think about Vince. The first time she'd seen him, he wore all black, combat boots, cargo pants, tank top and cap. His eyes were hidden behind dark glasses but his form was impressive. He was broad, lean and so very muscular. His bare arms were a tangle of muscle and sinew. His chest was a brick wall. His face was like stone. He never smiled or spoke. In fact, she'd never heard his voice until she ran into him at Pure, a nightclub, and even then she had no idea the handsome man in the silk suit with the velvet voice was the same man she'd lusted for at the Camp. If she had, she never would have run away and hooked up with the handsome Italian, Angelo.

Of course, that velvet voice could turn to sandpaper at the pull of a trigger. Sarah learned that lesson quickly enough during their first mission when she'd shot two pirates that tried to board the team's yacht in the Mediterranean.

It didn't matter. There was chemistry between them that couldn't be denied. Sarah knew it but it was so easy to fall back into her old insecurities from before her transformation at the Camp when she was the overweight, doormat always getting tossed aside by the men in her life. A wave of disgust threatened to overtake her whenever she thought about the way the old Sarah set her life aside for the men in her life. She couldn't deny her feelings for Vince, but she couldn't act on them either.

No hunk of beefcake is worth losing all this. My home and car are paid for, and my paycheck is a small fortune.

She couldn't afford not to focus on the job. It's just too dangerous when bullets are flying. That's what she kept telling herself but there was something inside her that just wouldn't give up the thought of someday being with him.

Until then, I'll just console myself with the good life.

Sarah reached up after her last stroke to grab the rail and climb out of the pool when, like a genie from a bottle, Vince was there. His hand caught hers as she took a breath.

"Good morning." He smiled that broad, white smile that always made her stomach flutter.

Sarah did her best to act cool but she was suddenly weak in the knees.

Vince caught her as she stumbled. "Too much yacht life. Looks like you aren't used to solid land yet."

Oh, God, he smells good enough to eat.

Sarah took a step back as she righted herself. "Long time no see.'

His eyes shined as he wiped his wet hands on his jeans. "Aw, did you miss me?"

Sarah tingled under his admiring gaze. She tried her best to act nonchalant. "Not really. I did miss Will though. Is he back, too?"

Vince took a deep breath and watched as Sarah dried off and wrapped the towel around her waist. "Uh, yeah." He looked away and surveyed the pool area. "He got in late yesterday. He's sleeping off the jet lag. You guys manage to stay out of trouble while we were gone?"

"Yeah, it's been quiet since we got back from our little trip to Mexico.

Talk about rest and relaxation. Brian's place in Cabo is gorgeous. As soon as we got back to Vegas, the Hawaiian Tropic girls came to town. Brian's house has been sticky with those broads for weeks." Sarah rolled her eyes sarcastically.

"Place probably stinks of coconut." He chuckled as he leaned back on a chaise. "So what's the tally? How many hearts have you broken?"

Sarah shrugged and shook her head. "Not a one." She had the body now and knew how to use it but clubbing for sex just wasn't her thing.

"Hey, Killer, I saw you reel in Hassan. You can't tell me you're not pulling in guys all the time."

She smiled and ran her fingers through her long, wet hair. "I'm telling you now. Hassan was just part of the mission. I don't waste my precious personal time with losers."

"Well, we're not all losers…" He smiled as he laced his fingers together and placed his hands under his head.

"No, you aren't all losers, but then again, you're not all available, are you?" Sarah pulled on her tunic. If she didn't get a few inches between them, she'd end up blurting that she was in love with him.

Fat lot of good that would do me. Hell, it would just screw up the team, my job, my life. No thanks!

He pulled himself up from his reclining position on the chaise. "Look, Sarah, there's something I gotta tell you."

He never calls me Sarah. This must be serious.

Sarah steeled herself and looked him in the eyes. He was still her boss.

"What is it?"

Vince looked down at his hands and fidgeted. "Uh…" Vince stalled. "Aw, forget it."

Why does he look so nervous?

She lowered her head and tried to connect with Vince's downcast eyes.

"Vince?"

After a pause, he raised his head cheerfully, "Oh, hey, Tracy says hello."

What is he afraid to say? When did he see Tracy?

Sarah smiled with a happy relief at hearing about her. Tracy had been Sarah's bunkmate at the Camp. They met in Phase I and trained together until they were both picked for teams within Task Force One-Twenty-Five. They'd run into each other briefly in London when they were both en route to their first missions. After a night of drinking and talking, they promised to stay in touch, but both knew it was difficult at best, with Tracy assigned to the former Soviet bloc and Sarah assigned to the area in and around the Mediterranean.

"Yeah? You went all the way out there, huh? How's she doing?"

"She's good. Their team is really gelling."

"Gelling, huh? That's good. And how about our team? Are we *gelling*

yet?"

Sarah sat on a nearby chaise, facing Vince.

He looked meaningfully at Sarah and spoke in a soft, low voice. "I'd say we passed gelling quite some time ago." He reached into his jacket pocket.

"That reminds me, here." He handed her a black box.

"What's this?"

Jewelry?

"Just a little something I thought you should have."

Sarah looked at the gold writing on the box.

Mikimoto.

15

She opened it carefully. "My pearls!" Sarah found herself looking at the

necklace she'd lost on their last mission.

"Not the same ones. There isn't a transmitter in these."

"You mean they're just jewelry, not government issue?"

"Yeah, just jewelry." He paused. "Just from me."

Sarah was stunned and grabbed Vince's hand. "Oh, my God, Vince. I...I don't know what to say."

Don't cry. Don't cry. Don't cry.

He held her free hand in both of his. "Don't say anything. I owed you for saving my ass. Consider this a 'thank you.' Let's just keep it between us though. After all, I don't buy the guys presents."

Vince seemed uncomfortable again.

"Ah-hah! Special treatment because I'm a girl, huh?" Sarah tried to lighten the mood.

"No, special treatment because you're such a damned good kisser."

Oh, God. You could revive the dead with your kisses.

There was that smile again. "We still have some unfinished business you know." He leaned closer.

There's that charm. So, it was the jewelry that made him nervous.

Sarah took a deep breath in an attempt to still the butterflies in her stomach as she looked into Vince's eyes. "I know."

Kiss me. Kiss me now.

"Hey, Vince! You're back! It's about time, man!"

The moment was lost and Vince jerked upright like a kid caught playing in class.

Sarah looked up and smiled at Brian Allen, the lean, tanned man with black hair and brown eyes who had just totally cock-blocked her. The six-foot-three, ex Navy SEAL was difficult to miss. This morning he was wearing black slacks, a tan dress shirt with the sleeves rolled up and the shadow of a beard.

He was carrying two cups of coffee and had a sleepy smile that led Sarah to conclude he'd gone clubbing, spent the night with a honey at the hotel, and was nursing a bit of a hangover. His shirt was only buttoned halfway and wasn't tucked into his pants. The shadow on his face gave away the fact he hadn't shaved since yesterday, and his hair looked liked it hadn't been combed yet.

Brian was the kind of guy who was so sexy and confident he was never at a loss when it came to picking up women. They'd flock around him even on his worst day. That's why Brian found it so easy to be such a womanizer. There was never a second date with him—a good thing in their line of work, though.

Brian was the best at what he did. He was the team's explosives expert, the man they counted on to blow things up, completely and on time. They didn't need his mind wandering when they were counting on him.

"Hey, you brought coffee!" Vince stood, greeted Brian and reached for a cup.

Brian pulled back. "Sorry, man. When you only have one drink to spare, do you give it to your buddy or to the hottie next to him?"

"No brainer." Vince conceded as he sat back down on the chaise.

Brian winked at Sarah. "Looking good, darlin'. Sorry I missed the bikini."

Sarah reached for the coffee Brian offered and smiled. "Strong coffee and two gorgeous men. This is how I should start every day, but," she stroked his chin, "it looks like *you're* still running on yesterday's sleep." Sarah took a sip of coffee and handed the cup to Vince. As their fingers touched, a spark shot straight up her spine, and she noticed that he held the contact a little longer than he should have.

Vince took a drink and passed it back.

Brian leaned against a table and nodded to Vince. "So how was the trip?"

"Good. We got a meeting with the Ukrainian next month in Italy."

"Yes, yes, of course you did." Brian rolled his eyes. "You always get what you want out of those people. But did you get laid?"

"Not that kind of trip, Bri."

"Every trip is that kind of trip! Well, we'll take care of that. We should all go out tonight. Maybe we can hook you up with some hot, blond actress wannabe." He raised his eyebrows suggestively.

"No thanks, man. I'm getting tired of blond one-nighters."

"You? No way."

"Yeah, the ex definitely turned me off to blonds. I think it's time I find a different type."

Brian grinned at Sarah and looked her over. "Too bad Sarah worked out so well on the team. She's the only one I know who's woman enough to handle you."

Vince looked at his shoes. "Yeah, you know, maybe we should all go out tonight. Whaddya say, Sarah?"

"I have a date, but I can probably meet you guys later." The last thing

Sarah wanted to do was watch Vince pick up some bimbo at a Las Vegas nightclub, but she knew the score. They both needed to keep their heads clear and their relationship totally platonic. The blind date with her Russian tutor's son was the first date she'd accepted since Hassan. It was time to get back in the saddle whether she wanted to or not.

It's about time I get Hassan and Vince out of my head.

Vince gave Sarah a sideways glance as she handed the coffee cup back to him. "A date, huh? Who's the lucky guy?"

"Nobody special. My tutor's son."

Vince slipped into interrogation mode. "What tutor? Agency or civilian?"

"Civilian. It's no big deal. I've been working on my Russian since we got back, and she thought I might get along well with her son. It is just practice in a social situation. I thought it would mix things up so I agreed."

Brian noticed the pearls in the box on the table near Sarah. "Hey, where did you get those? You weren't wearing those when you jumped off Hassan's boat." His eyes sparkled. "Matter of fact you weren't wearing much at all when we pulled you out of the drink." A silly smile rolled across Brian's face as he looked up at nothing in particular. "God, I love my job."

Sarah smiled and exhaled a silent sigh of relief at Brian's change in topic. "Brian, there are just some things in life a girl doesn't want to live without once she's had a taste."

Vince smiled meaningfully as he passed the coffee cup back to her.

"Yeah, I get that all the time." Brian deadpanned. "Well, I'd love to stay here and shoot the breeze, but I need some breakfast. You guys coming?"

Vince rolled his shoulders. "No, I need a shower and some sleep."

"I think I'll pass, Bri. Thanks."

"Suit yourselves. I'll see you guys later."

Sarah and Vince walked into their building and stepped onto the elevator.

Vince pushed the button for Sarah's floor, two stories above his. "You do have coffee up there, don't you? I haven't had a chance to do groceries since I moved in."

"Absolutely." Sarah nodded.

God help me.

They walked into Sarah's apartment.

"It's been a long night on planes. Do you mind if I shower while you make coffee?"

Not if you don't mind if I join you.

Before Sarah could answer, Vince walked into her bathroom and turned on the shower. If it had been any of the other guys on the team, it wouldn't have phased her one bit, but the fact Vince was naked and in her apartment was killing her. She tried to distract herself by making a pot of coffee and a couple of omelets.

The smell of the coffee brewing and the eggs frying triggered Sarah's hunger. Her stomach growled and rumbled. Distracted at seeing Vince again, she'd forgotten how hungry she was. She plated the two Denver omelets and placed them on the table, then poured two cups of black coffee. Vince strolled out of her bedroom with nothing but a towel wrapped around his trim waist, his ripped chest and abs caused her to stop mid step. For all the traveling he did, he never went without a workout or ate poorly. His heavily muscled body was always cut to shreds.

How can it be my job demands me to bed men I could easily hate but never touch the one man I could probably love? Fate is a cruel bitch.

A knock on Sarah's door dragged her back to reality. She was so flustered she practically forgot where the door was!

Brian bounced in. "Hey, Sarah, remembering you wet and in your underwear had me so distracted I forgot I didn't drive last night." Then

Brian saw Vince walk to the table and sit down in nothing but a towel. "Hey, glad I caught you, man. Let me borrow your truck. I'll bring it back tonight."

"Sure, man. Keys are in my jacket on the bed."

"Cool." Brian strode into the bedroom, as Sarah stood there dumb with the coffee pot in one hand and a cup of coffee in the other. "Thanks, man. See you guys later."

When Brian closed the door, Sarah turned her shock to Vince. "Do you realize what he's going to think?"

Vince took his cup of coffee from Sarah and grinned. "What? That in the time it took for him to hit the lobby and then walk back here I'd had my way with you, taken a shower, made the bed and sat down to a breakfast you had time to cook?" He smiled softly at Sarah. "Honey, I take my time. And, with you, I'd savor every second. I wouldn't have even finished the foreplay in that amount of time."

Her body tingled with his imagined touch. She realized how ridiculous she was being and sat down. "Well, I hope not."

Neither spoke as they ate.

Sarah tried to focus on her breakfast instead of pushing Vince into the bedroom and thanking him properly for the pearls.

Vince finished his omelet and brought his dish to the sink. Sarah stayed seated at the table with her back to the kitchen and finished her coffee.

"Sarah, we need to talk."

A chill shot up Sarah's spine and erased every fantasy of thanking him for the pearls. She closed her eyes, willing the conversation away. "About what?"

"There has always been chemistry between us."

Oh, crap! Not the "I know you have a crush on me, get over it" talk.

Sarah stood and set her dishes in the sink. Standing directly in front of Vince and close enough to feel the heat from his body, she looked him in the eyes and lied a little. "Honey, I've got chemistry with everybody. That's my job.

Don't take it personally."

If I can't be with him, I still want to be able to be around him. I can't risk getting kicked off the team.

He reached for her and ran his fingertips down her arms. "Do you?"

Oh, sweet Jesus. Take me now!

Sarah bit her bottom lip and looked at Vince's forehead so she wouldn't have to look into his eyes when she lied. "It's what I do."

Vince smiled. "Okay, cool. There is a lot at stake here, and we all need to bring our A-games."

"Oh, I'm bringing it." She smiled to lighten the mood. "Believe it or not, I'm not going to jump anybody on the team just because they're easy." Sarah turned and busied herself with the dishes. Looking at Vince standing there in a towel was too much.

"What? Are you saying I'm easy?"

"If the towel fits."

Vince chuckled. "I wish I'd met you years ago. Things might have been different."

Sarah smiled and blinked back the mist forming over her eyes. "That's sweet for a tough guy, but you know you wouldn't have done anything differently. What you see here is a product of the mission. I've never been a beauty. You never would have noticed me."

"I don't know about that. You're a hard one to miss."

Sarah turned to look at Vince. He was the most attractive man she'd ever laid eyes on. Every inch of her screamed to touch him. It would be so easy just to pull that towel from his waist, but there was too much on the line and she couldn't mess it up by complicating things with sex and emotions.

She cleared her throat. "You'd better get downstairs and get some sleep."

"I'm gonna go get dressed."

Sarah looked Vince over and took a deep breath through her teeth. She couldn't help but smile at him. "Yeah, I think you should." She caught a glimpse of a smile as he looked down and walked away.

A few minutes later, Vince emerged from the bedroom fully dressed and headed for the door. He spoke over his shoulder. "Thanks for breakfast.

Mission brief tomorrow at oh-nine-hundred. Usual place."

Sarah walked toward the door after him. "I'll be there."

"I'll see you later tonight." He leaned in and kissed her softly on the lips.

A jolt arced through Sarah's body like she just stuck her finger in a two-hundred-twenty volt socket. Her heart stopped.

"I, uh, I'm sorry. I don't know where that came from."

That was the first time Sarah saw Vince nervous. She caught the gleam of panic in his eyes and gathered enough self-control to let him off the hook.

Too many mixed signals, Sarah. It's too dangerous. Let it go.

"You're just tired. Go get some rest."

He sighed. "You're a good sport, Sarah."

"Not the first time I've heard that."

Good sport. Doormat. Same. Same.

Vince stopped short and turned to look at Sarah on his way out the door.

"Sarah, I'm not that guy."

"I know, Vince."

You can't help it. Your personal life will always be second to the mission.

Four

"Vince, check it out." Will nodded in the direction of the bar.

Vince turned to see Sarah in a very short dress, standing near the bar with a man's arm around her waist and liking it. The guy wore an Armani suit and was flashing a killer smile at her every chance he could. It made Vince's skin crawl to see her with somebody else.

Get a grip on yourself, man. She's not yours.

He turned back to the table and drank his beer in one long gulp. "So she's having a drink with a guy. So what? The girl's not a machine." He said the words more for himself than for Will, and he wasn't buying any of it. He never had a problem separating his business from his personal life, but Sarah changed all of that.

"Yeah, I'm on board with that but take a closer look at the guy."

Sarah's date turned around at that moment and Vince suddenly realized the cause for Will's concern. "You gotta be shitting me!"

Will shook his head. "I want to chalk this up to a small world but that's just too small."

No fucking way!

Vince stood up and walked directly to the man with his hand on Sarah's hip. "Well, I'll be damned!" He gave Nikolai a light, one-armed hug as he shook his hand.

No guns.

Nikolai smiled as he checked Vince for a weapon the same way. It was the standard underworld greeting when you weren't expecting to see someone who made their living selling weapons. "Vince. What a surprise. What are you doing here?"

Wondering what the hell you're doing with your arm around my honey pot!

"Everybody likes business meetings in Las Vegas." Vince waved to the bartender who nodded back as he poured about twenty cosmopolitans for a squealing bunch of hotties who, by the look of the one in the veil, were having a bachelorette party. "Fancy meeting you here." He gave Sarah a quick glance as though he didn't know her before moving between her and Nikolai and dismissing her.

I don't want this slimeball close enough to touch you.

"Hey, sweetheart. Excuse us for a minute?"

~~~

Sarah stepped away into the crowd but kept her eyes on Vince. She wasn't sure what the hell was going on between him and Nikolai, but she was pretty certain she wouldn't be getting anywhere near lucky tonight.

Will emerged from the crowd of partygoers and smiled at Sarah as he took her arm. "Let me buy you a drink." He kept a firm grip on her arm and pulled her into the crowd of squealing girls at the other end of the long bar in the elegant White Room at Pure. When Vince and Nikolai were out of sight, Will stopped and his tone seemed almost interrogative. "Sarah, what are you doing here? Do you know who this guy is? Where did you meet him?"

Sarah gripped her purse tight and clenched her teeth.

What the hell? After his speech about A-games this morning, he's got the balls to bring Will in on crashing my date?

"Being a bit overprotective, aren't you? Am I not allowed to date? Nobody ever said I wasn't allowed to have a life off duty." She glared at Will and spoke with an edge of indignation in her voice. "Did you guys follow me here?"

Will's blue eyes focused on hers, icy cold. "Sarah, tell me how you met this guy."

"He's Niko, my Russian tutor's son."

Will flipped open his phone and hit a speed dial number. "Your tutor?

Your tutor set this up?"

Going a little overboard about a date, aren't we?

"Yeah, why? There's no policy that says I can't see men outside the job.

What's this about?"

"You can't see this guy again."

Sarah stopped smiling and glared at Will.

Where the hell do these guys get off telling me I can't go out for dinner and drinks with someone?

"Why not?"

Will held the phone to his ear and raised his hand motioning for Sarah to stop. He spoke quickly into the phone. "Chris, you need to run a background on Sarah's tutor." Will's jaw was firm and his eyes narrowed when he looked at Sarah again. "Did the agency set up the tutor?"

"No, she's a civilian from the University of Nevada."

"She's a civilian, Chris. Get a complete background."

I need to have the fucking CIA do background checks on my dates?

"What the hell? Since when do I need a background check for a dinner date? It's not like I'm shacking up with the guy."

This is Vince's doing. He doesn't want me, but he doesn't want anybody else to have me either. Like a dog pissing on a tree.

"This is bullshit."

What started as an innocent date and some great Russian practice turned into a load of bullshit with the Cock-of-the-Walk.

Will smiled at Sarah. "Just pretend you don't know who we are."

Sarah turned on her heel to make her way back to the bar and Niko. "I don't."

Vince smiled politely at Sarah as she returned through the crowd. "Sorry to interrupt your evening." The bartender finally arrived and Vince ordered with a pat on Nikolai's shoulder. "Your best champagne for my friend, Nikolai. Put it on my tab."

The bartender nodded. "Sure, Vince. I'll have it brought to their table."

Sarah smiled at Niko. "A friend of yours?"

"A business associate." He slipped a hand around her waist and led her through the crowd. "Our table is in the Red Room. Let's get out of this crowd and drink that champagne."

What kind of associate? If he was a bad guy, Vince and Will would have whisked me out of here. Wouldn't they?

Sarah had enjoyed her date with Niko up until Will and Vince interrupted. She had some difficulty getting back in the festive, flirty mood they'd been in previously. Anger at Vince's mixed messages festered inside her.

After a glass of champagne and some small talk, Niko's phone rang. He pulled the phone from his breast pocket. "Excuse me?"

Sarah nodded politely, grateful for the interruption.

25

"Yes? Oh, really?" He turned to look at Sarah and he wasn't smiling.

A chill went up Sarah's spine.

Okay, I am definitely uncomfortable now.

"No, there's no need for that. Yes, I'll take care of it right now." He slipped his phone back into his pocket and fidgeted with his tie.

Sarah smiled demurely. "Is everything okay?"

"Unfortunately, no. I need to take care of some business tonight. I'm sorry to cut this short. I'll take you home."

"Thank you but there is no need. I'll just take a taxi."

"I insist." He stood. "The city at night can be a dangerous place. I'd never forgive myself if something happened to you on your way home."

"No, really. I'll be fine." Something about the way he looked at her made Sarah feel uneasy so she told a little lie. "I have to stop to get some cat food anyway." She hated cats.

Niko walked her out of the crowded club and saw her to a taxi.

She kissed him lightly on the cheek. "Thank you for a lovely evening."

"I'll be in town for a few more days. May I call you tomorrow?"

He'll never call. Something is really wrong here and I plan to get to the bottom of it right now.

Sarah kept her cool and smiled. "I'll look forward to it."

Those bastards cock blocked me and that call was his way of getting out of a bad date.

~~~

Sarah walked into her apartment and closed the door. She pulled her phone out of her purse and dialed Vince.

No answer.

Those sons of bitches are going to answer for this.

The more Sarah thought about it, the angrier she became.

Where the hell do they get off scaring my dates away like a couple of big brothers puffing up their chests?

She called Will.

He picked up on the first ring. "Sarah, you okay?"

"I'm pissed. Where's Vince?"

"We left the club about fifteen minutes ago. He was going straight back to his place."

"Great. I'll find him."

"Sa..."

Sarah hung up before he could say anything. She left her apartment, stomped down the hallway and punched the elevator button.

Son of a bitch.

When the elevator didn't show up immediately, she ripped open the stairwell door and ran down the two flights of stairs to Vince's floor.

She banged on his apartment door like a cop ready to bust a drug dealer.

Vince opened the door within seconds wearing a casual smile. "Hey, sweetheart."

A flash of pink silk caught Sarah's eye. She looked past Vince to see a beautiful brunette in pajamas lounging on his sofa.

Rage boiled beneath her skin. Every muscle in her body tensed with anger. She glared at him but he seemed oblivious as he smiled at her.

Mutherfucker!

She didn't try to stop herself as she threw her whole body into a hard punch to his stomach.

Vince wasn't expecting the hit. He braced his hands on the doorframe, bent slightly into himself and stepped back before recovering. His face was red and he looked genuinely surprised when he looked up.

His voice boomed. "What the hell was that for?"

"Don't sweetheart me, you bastard! You get to bring women home whenever you like, but I finally find a nice guy to go out to dinner with and you and your flunky, Will, have to fuck it up?"

He shook his head and grabbed her arm. "Now hold on a minute!"

Sarah cut him off. "No, *you* hold on!" She shook her arm free of his grip.

"Let's get something clear here. We may work together but my off-duty time is mine." Sarah turned without waiting for a response and stormed down the hall. Behind her, she heard Vince's door slam shut.

Son of a bitch!

~~~

Vince slammed the door and stalked across the room to the bar.

"*Damnit!*" He poured a drink and then pounded the bottle of Jameson so hard it shattered on the bar. "Bitch!"

27

"Wow! Vinny's in love."

He shot a glare at the pretty brunette and raised his hand for her to stop. "Don't start, Gina." He flopped onto the couch, set his drink down and lit a cigarette.

Gina walked over to the bar and started picking up the broken glass.

"That was a good bottle of Irish whiskey. Dad would have your ass for alcohol abuse like that."

Vince slugged his whiskey and shot another glare at Gina.

She smiled. "You were right. She is pretty." Gina giggled like she'd just been tickled. "I like her spunk. She's a keeper, bro. I don't know what happened tonight but you should go talk to her."

Vince growled at Gina. "I don't feel much like talking right now."

She gingerly tossed a handful of broken glass into the garbage can.

"Okay. I get it. Nobody likes getting sucker punched and told off. Kinda like growing up with Rig and Marco, huh?"

Vince smiled at the reference to his brothers. They all used to give each other some hard beatings as kids. He pulled his phone out of his pocket and dialed Will.

"Hey, boss. Sarah's lookin' for you."

"She found me. What did you tell her about Nikolai?"

"She didn't give me a chance to tell her anything. Why?"

Vince rolled his eyes. "That explains it."

"Did you fill her in on Nikolai?"

"Nope. She didn't give me a chance either."

"Oh, well. She's safe?"

"Yeah, safe as a junkyard dog." Vince hung up and set his phone on the table in front of him.

Shit.

Five

Sarah woke up still pissed from the night before and continued to chew on her anger as she drove out to the desert. After their talk yesterday morning, she really thought she and Vince were on the same page. Sure, they couldn't be together, but she didn't think Vince would do anything as juvenile as cock block her before bringing some bimbo back to his place.

What kind of guy does that?

To bring Will in on it was just beyond comprehension. Even if Vince was that big of a prick, she never expected that sort of behavior from Will.

A cloud of dust followed behind her as she drove along the dry, dusty roads toward the Camp. When she reached the secret CIA training base, she pulled up under a canopy of camouflage fabric and parked her Jeep before going into the briefing hut.

The rest of the team filed into the room shortly after she took a chair at the briefing table. Once they were all seated, Colonel Young, their team's handler, came in and began the briefing.

"You folks did a great job of taking out Hassan and his network. We seized so much money Al Qaeda is definitely feeling the pinch. Unfortunately, there are always people happy to raise more. Now we have to hit them where it really hurts, their supply lines."

"No guns, no war."

"That's right, Jason." Young picked up a remote from the table and clicked on a large television screen. "Vince and Will have been working their network since your last mission and cut a deal with a major arms player, Nikolai Federov."

Sarah caught her breath as she looked up at the familiar face on the screen. He had longer hair and a beard, but it was him. The hairs on the back of her neck stood up and her skin went cold. She gasped. She looked over at Vince, and he shot her a sideways glare.

Oh, shit.

Sarah's face grew hot with shame. She'd punched out her boss for breaking up her date with a major arms dealer.

This is so not good.

Young continued and flashed another face on the screen. "Victor Bolshoi is the best at what he does. Nobody thinks about getting into the arms trade without first considering how it may affect him. So far as we know, he is the Godfather of arms traders. The real power player. Nobody makes a move without his blessing. Victor has the infrastructure to move anything, anywhere. He also has a virtually unlimited supply of Soviet light and heavy weapons as well as delivery vehicles to include aircraft, watercraft and land vehicles."

Sarah examined the photo closely.

Brian winced. "One stop shopping, eh?"

"That's right. If you want to go to war, you call Victor. Even if you don't call Victor and get your supplies from another dealer, that dealer will have to call Victor because he's the only one who can move merchandise from point A to point B. He is your next target."

My new boyfriend. And to think I was only one degree of separation off.

Ain't that some shit?

Young placed the remote on the table and walked around the room to pass out mission folders to all of the team members. "He has more than a handful of legitimate import-export businesses and is so good at hiding his tracks, nobody has been able to get anything to stick. The Belgians tried it once but he slipped through their system in twenty-four hours. The Italians have been trying to nail him for years but never get enough evidence to hold him. They're going to work with us on this operation. Your team needs to infiltrate and get enough information so we can finally nail him to the wall.

Since we have a special arrangement with the Italians and what we're doing isn't exactly legal over there, they, of course, will receive the credit if the job goes well."

Chris opened the folder placed in front of him. "But won't that destabilize the international arms trade and create a vacuum for even more small players to rise up?"

Young nodded. "Yes, it will." He crossed his arms over his huge chest.

"That's why we're counting on you to find information on everyone he does business with. With that, we can coordinate with other agencies and pick everyone up in one fell swoop. With all the key players out of the game, it is going to make things very difficult for the small time dealers to move anything.

That should buy us enough time and enough advantage to put the pressure on

Al Qaeda." Young picked up his coffee and took a drink. "No guns. No ammo.

No war."

Brian spoke up. "This guy is in his thirties?"

Will smiled at Brian and nodded.

"He's pulling in some serious money." Brian set the financial analysis back in his folder. "Damn. I'm in the wrong business."

Young paced like he always did when he was briefing. "Don't let his age fool you. He's young but he's smart. He graduated from the Military Institute of Foreign Languages in Moscow. He's got at least five passports and twice as many aliases. He's language-smart. He speaks Russian, Farsi, Arabic, English, French, Portuguese, Spanish, Italian, Xhosa and Zulu that we know of. His only weaknesses are his cocaine habit and his need to have lots of women around, most of whom are paid well to be there."

Will and Jason turned and smiled at Sarah.

She shot them a confident nod and turned her attention back to Young.

Chris looked up from the page he was reading in the folder. "If we've got all this shit on him, why haven't we just snagged him and made him disappear?"

Young's face turned serious. "Let's just say that, until recently, he's been useful and leave it at that. They're all yours, Major Hennessee."

Vince sat back in his chair and continued the briefing seated.

Every time he made eye contact with Sarah, she looked down at the folder in front of her. She was so ashamed of what she'd done she couldn't bear to look at him. She was still pissed about the fact he'd brought a woman home with him, but then that made her no better than she'd assumed of him. The shame doubled.

The briefing ended an hour later.

31

"Okay, that's it, people." Vince closed the folder in front of him. "Go home and pack your bags. We leave for Italy tomorrow at oh-seven-hundred."

Sarah couldn't get out of there fast enough and jumped out of her seat.

Vince's large hand came down on her shoulder and pushed her back into her chair. "Stevens. You stay for a few minutes."

Oh, man. Here it comes. Shame, shame, shame.

Sarah looked up at Vince's brown eyes. They were usually so soft and warm. Today they were hard and cold. "Look, Vince, I didn't know. I…"

"Shut up."

Sarah was so surprised by his harsh tone and the words he used she did exactly that.

He looked at the door as it closed. He spoke once he heard it latch. "The last person who sucker punched me woke up in a hospital bed."

Sarah shook her head. "I was out of line."

Vince jumped in before she said any more. "You're damned right you were out of line! Do you think this is a game?" He continued before she could answer. "We're not a bunch of kids playing spies here. This is the real deal, Stevens. We've got better things to do than bust up your dates."

"I…"

"Be quiet! If you want to stay on this team, you're going to have to learn to trust us. You need to trust me. The way you see things isn't always the way they are."

All she could see was the grain of the wood on the conference table and she desperately wanted to be the tiny, light, speck under her hand. Shame over her behavior and humiliation over the dressing down she was receiving created a burning desire to get out of that room and as far away from Vince as she could. She slipped into military mode to escape and leave as soon as possible. "Yes, sir."

"Now do you have anything to say?"

Yeah. Fuck you. You should have told me what was going on.

"Yes, sir. My behavior was ill informed, over-reactive and unprofessional. It won't happen again."

And fuck you.

"That's it?"

Oh, yeah. I almost forgot. Fuck you.

"Yes, sir."

Vince leaned in over Sarah's left shoulder. His aftershave was faint, musky and delicious, and she hated that the very scent of him made her weak.

"I get that you have trust issues, but I'm not one of your ex boyfriends playing games here. I'm the one guy you *can* trust because I'd rather take a bullet than see you hurt. I'm your guardian fucking angel. Lucky me!" Vince pushed his chair in with so much force it crashed and slid under the table. He didn't give it a second glance as he walked out of the room.

His sarcasm stung. She knew the punch last night wasn't about her date being blown. It was because he had another woman in his room. A brunette.

I'm a brunette. A jealous brunette.

The thing with Niko didn't piss her off nearly as much as that brunette did.

You gotta stop thinking about this man. No matter how much you want him, it's never going to happen.

Sarah drove back to her apartment and started packing.

Six

Sarah drove to the Camp to meet the rest of the team for their transport to the airport. Vince and Will were already there.

Will smiled. "Morning, pork chop."

Vince stayed silent.

Sarah wanted to just run into Vince's arms and tell him how much she hated that he was seeing other women, but there was no way.

Not in this world. Not in this lifetime.

She smiled at Will. "Morning, Will. Good morning, Major Hennessee."

Will squinted and shot Vince a questioning glance. Sarah's formal address to Vince wasn't lost on him.

Sarah assumed Will was in on everything Vince did, but he obviously wasn't aware of their exchange after the briefing.

It doesn't matter. I'm here to do a job. Getting all hot and bothered about Vince just gets in the way anyway.

Jason, Brian and Chris pulled up and the rush of activity began, transferring gear from their cars to the two big, black, Suburbans they'd drive to the airport. After they loaded all the gear and luggage, Sarah hopped into one of the Suburbans with Brian, Jason and Chris.

Chris squinted over at her from across the back seat and handed Sarah her earpiece. Once they'd tested them to be sure they were both transmitting to and receiving from each other, he spoke in Russian. "What's wrong, Sarah?"

Everything.

"Nothing."

"You're quiet. You're never quiet. You're sitting in your seat like a dog that's been kicked. You're riding with us instead of Will and Vince. It doesn't take an intelligence analyst to see something is wrong here, so spill it, sister."

He's got a point.

"I screwed up. I went off on Vince for busting up that date I had. '

"You mean your date with the Russian arms dealer?" Chris chuckled.

Anger bubbled inside her and she growled at Chris. "Nobody told me he was a Russian arms dealer."

"He didn't tell you who Nikolai was?"

"Nope."

"So you thought…?"

"Yep. I went off half-cocked and kinda told him off."

Chris raised his eyebrows in curiosity. "*Kinda,* like how?"

"There may have been a one-sided physical altercation."

"Oh, my God." Chris sniggered into his hand. "You hit him?"

Sarah rolled her eyes.

"Well, I guess that explains his foul mood."

"Do you think he'll kick me off the team?"

"Oh, hell no. The team is like a family—for better or for worse. Besides, he's crazy about you."

Sarah wrinkled her brow. "Huh?"

"We're men but we're not stupid. The man has it bad for you."

"Can't be so bad. He had a pretty brunette in his apartment when I told

him off."

Chris laughed out loud and shook his head. "You're just as bad as he is! You need to talk to him when we get to Italy."

Fat lot of good that will do.

Sarah's thoughts were interrupted when Jason turned around and grinned at her from the front passenger seat. "I know you're speaking Russian but all I understand are the bad words. If you aren't going to talk dirty then we'd appreciate it if you girls did your dishing in English from now on so we can eavesdrop properly."

~~~

No one spoke until the private plane transporting the team to Italy was in the air.

Vince broke the silence. "Okay, you're probably wondering why we're staging so early for this operation in Italy. We're going to set up our base of operations on an estate near Victor's place in Sori. We'll be staying as houseguests of a member of the Gruppo di Intervento Speciale or G.I.S. We've been assured it is secure and instructed that it will serve as our base of operations while we're in country."

Brian spoke up. "Hey, man, I know the G.I.S. is pretty bad ass, but I've never heard anything about them being paid well enough to have country estates."

Chris chimed in. "We've had a full check done on this guy. He's from old money and had an exemplary career in the G.I.S. There's no chance he's on the take."

Brian sat back in his seat. "Cool. What else do we know about the guy?"

Chris looked at Vince. "I just got the rip on him last night."

Vince nodded to Chris to continue.

"They call him the Dark Angel." Chris ran his fingers through his shiny blonde curls. "This guy has done anti-terror ops all over the globe. He's been doing this for almost thirty years now. He's very highly decorated. Whenever the G.I.S. has a tough job, they send him. They say he's the best."

Jason took a swig of the coffee he'd brought with him. "Boss, you've been doing this a while. Have you worked with this superstar? Do we know him personally?"

Vince shook his head. "Not me. Will?"

Will shrugged. "I've heard stories about a Dark Angel. I thought they were just urban legend. Based on the stories, I'm pretty sure we'd know if we had met him."

Chris' mouth curled into a wry smile. "Now that you mention it, Sarah knows him."

Oh, come on! How many surprises do I need in a single week?

Sarah sat up straight in her seat. "Huh?"

Chris nodded to Sarah. "Seems he was in Las Vegas a little while back."

Vince glared at Sarah. "Jesus Christ, Stevens." He rubbed his forehead. "Will and I take off for a few weeks and you're out dating both sides in the war? Who the hell else have you got in your little black book?"

Of course. Now he thinks I'm playing both sides. Frigging great.

Sarah rolled her eyes and adjusted in her seat so she didn't have to look at Vince. "Look, Chris, I don't know where you got your information but it's wrong." She stood and started walking to the bathroom. She glared at Vince as she walked by his seat. "I've been on one date since Hassan and you know exactly how that went." Sarah walked into the bathroom and slammed the door before sitting down and wiping what would soon be a tear from her eye.

Chris' voice came through her earpiece. "Now wait a minute, Vince. This was before she was assigned to us, when she was still a civilian at the Camp.

She met Angelo socially at Pure while she was on a twenty-four-hour pass."

Angelo? Oh, boy.

Sarah heard Will's voice next and he didn't sound happy. "What the hell is going on with you, man? Why are you suddenly so hard on the girl? She hasn't done anything wrong, and she's pulled your ass out of the fire more than once. No disrespect, brother, but you need to pull that stick out of your ass and cut her some slack."

Silence. Bastard.

Sarah waited a few minutes, freshened up her makeup and then walked silently back to her seat next to Chris without making eye contact with Vince.

How did everything go to shit so quickly?

Chris gave her a sorry smile and mouthed the words, "You okay?"

Sarah nodded.

I punched a Marine in front of a woman. We may never get past that one. After all, a man's got his pride.

Will cleared his throat. "Chris, why don't you give us that brief on Bolshoi now so we can all get some sleep while we cross the pond?"

Sitting straight, Chris was all business as he rifled through the papers and folders in his briefcase. "So, from the intel we have, Bolshoi runs a maze of companies and employs upwards of four-hundred people. He's got anywhere from fifty to sixty operational aircraft at any given time and they're always moving. This guy has the largest private fleet of Soviet era cargo planes in the world."

"How do we know he's not just moving tulips from the Netherlands?"

Chris sighed and rolled his eyes. "Good question, Brian, what with the tulip trade being so lucrative and all."

Brian opened his hands as if to say, "It could happen."

Jason turned toward Will. "Soviet era? Is he connected?"

Will stretched his legs. "Our contacts in the Russian Mafia are sketchy at best, so we're just going to have to cross that bridge when we get to it."

"We've got lots of conjecture from the analysts and allegations by the U.N. but nothing solid to go on here." Chris looked up from his papers and spoke directly to Vince. "We're really bumping around in the dark on this guy.

I'm surprised they put us on him at this point."

Vince leaned back in his seat. "It was good intel from the case on Hassan. We can run with this. It shouldn't be a problem to nail him in a week or so. These guys never take vacations. We get Sarah in there, bug the phone lines, plant a few microphones and cameras, then cut the deal and we're out of there."

"I don't know, Vince." Chris protested. "There are mumblings this guy has ties to the director of Russia's Ministry of Internal Affairs. That guy was old school KGB. I advise we use extreme caution in this case."

"Thank you for your input on this, Chris, and I appreciate you doing your homework on Bolshoi but we've been given an assignment here. We can't exactly turn it down."

"Alright." Will walked to the bar and poured himself some coffee. "So we have an assignment and our guy has cautioned us about possible dangers. Everybody we work with is dangerous so let's just be smart and go into this with our eyes open and get the job done."

"What else have you got on Victor, Chris?"

"Nothing you didn't already know, boss. He's got heavy connections to Ernst Wagner."

Sarah looked up at Chris. "Who is that?"

Vince came as close to talking to Sarah as he had all day. "He was the agency's go-to guy for guns during the Cold War. The KGB used him a lot, too. If you ask me, he was the guy who won the Cold War. Son of a bitch made billions on it. He's retired in Monaco now, but no doubt has a Rolodex any gun runner would happily kill for."

~~~

After refueling in Boston for the transatlantic flight, the team settled in, and Sarah was ready to talk again. She nudged Chris.

He stopped tapping away on his laptop keyboard and smiled at her. "What's up?"

"Tell me about the G.I.S."

"The Italian Carabinieri do both civilian and military policing. Their training is very military and way tougher than any civilian cops get in the U.S.

Their elite counter-terrorism unit is called the Gruppo di Intervento Speciale or G.I.S. If a military base is under threat, or there is a terrorist attack, or they need a bunch of bad asses to deploy as peacekeepers, they send the G.I.S."

Chris leaned back in his seat. "These guys took on the Red Brigade and Sicilian Mafia and lived to tell about it." Chris seemed very impressed. "There are only a hundred guys in the G.I.S. They're selected only from the Carabinieri and they must have an outstanding military record and jump through some serious hoops just to try out for a spot. Their training and selection process is really tough. It's like two weeks of the SEALs Hell Week."

Brian was resting in the seat across the aisle from Sarah and perked up at the mention of SEALs. "Yeah, that ain't no frat party. Those G.I.S. guys are hard core."

~~~

As the team began their final approach to Christopher Columbus airport in Genoa, Vince made a phone call from the cabin of the jet. He spoke in Italian, and Sarah found herself drifting into happier thoughts as she listened to the lilt and roll of his voice speaking the language so fluently.

He sounded almost happy to hear from me when I called him in Pridnestrovie. He brought me that necklace. He kissed me.

Sarah snapped out of her daydream with a bump as they landed. She heard a helicopter overhead but didn't think anything of it.

Vince stood, walked to the door of the aircraft and looked at Sarah as he opened it. "Let's see what Sarah's Dark Angel looks like."

And there you are again, the world's biggest asshole.

The rest of the team filed out of the aircraft. Sarah was the last to step out.

The helicopter set down about a hundred yards from their plane. A man dressed completely in black stepped out. There he was, the Dark Angel. Sarah had forgotten how handsome he was. He wore black cargo pants, a black tee shirt and a black leather jacket.

What is it about all of the men in my new life? They are always in black.

Sarah had to admit, black certainly suited Angelo. He wore dark sunglasses and a Bluetooth earpiece. After the night they'd spent together in Las Vegas, meeting at a high-end nightclub and drinking champagne, it was odd for her to see him wired for the sort of work she'd never expected of him.

In fact, in light of Vince's recent behavior, Angelo looked downright hot. She smiled a sly grin as Angelo walked straight toward her, seemingly oblivious to the rest of the team standing with her.

Seven

He took both her hands in his. "So, this is the business that took you away from me? A showgirl or business woman I would have believed, but never a spy!" Angelo chuckled and kissed Sarah on both cheeks. "This is a pleasant surprise, *cara*."

The tension drained from her and she smiled. "Very pleasant."

Vince cleared his throat.

Sarah nearly forgot he was standing beside her.

Angelo reached his right hand over the left one that still held Sarah's and shook Vince's hand. "You must be Mr. Hennessee?"

"Major Hennessee." There wasn't even the hint of a polite smile on Vince's face as he scowled at Angelo.

~~~

"Welcome to Genova." Angelo opened the front door and ushered everyone into a very large, formal entryway. A huge round oak table sat in the middle of the spiral patterned marble floor.

Will let out a short sigh. "Angelo, I like your style."

A magnificent bouquet of long-stemmed white roses virtually exploded from the top of an eighteen inch, black marble vase.

Oh, my God! This place is fantastic!

On each side of the entry hall rose a flight of stairs leading to an open hallway along the second story. Angelo led them up one of the stairways and began showing them to their rooms. He opened the first door on the right. "There are two beds in this room and a full bath."

Jason and Chris claimed the room. As junior members of the team, they were accustomed to bunking together.

As the rest of the team walked down the hallway to the next room, Jason was heard gushing over his room. "A big screen and babes on the beach. I love this job!"

Angelo smiled and moved down the hallway, opening another door on the right. "Two beds and a full bath in here as well."

Brian and Will set their bags inside the door. Although they were all CIA, military protocols were accepted and expected from everyone on the team.

"Meet downstairs in thirty minutes." Vince spoke loud enough for Chris and Jason to hear him down the hall. Sarah noticed there was a bit more command in his voice than usual.

Is he still pissed about the punch? Get over it!

Sarah marveled at the view of the hall below as she and Vince continued to follow Angelo along the hall. Angelo opened the last door along the hall.

"Major Hennessee, you will have this room. The bath is to the left."

As Vince entered his room, Angelo took Sarah's hand and led her down a small hallway. "And you, *cara…*" Sarah walked into the most luxurious bedroom suite she'd ever seen.

~~~

Though the exterior of the house glowed with old world charm and history, the interior was rich and modern. The ornate tile floor showed a Moorish influence but was so well kept it looked as though it had been installed last week. The fireplace, framed in granite, had a hearth arranged with white pillar candles just waiting to be lit. Two large windows, covered in white gossamer and framed in green velvet, consumed the far wall. An antique writing desk faced one of the windows. A king sized bed done in green to match the curtains, with an ornately carved Italian Renaissance style headboard, lay against the east wall of the room. Just inside the room, a doorway led into a beautiful, white marble bathroom.

Sarah inhaled deeply as the sea breeze whispered through the windows and ruffled the delicate white curtains.

"Oh, Angelo! This is beautiful."

Angelo turned to face Sarah and wrapped his arms around her. "I'll be sleeping in the room adjoining my office downstairs. Please feel free to visit anytime." He kissed her cheek and whispered in her ear. "I'd be lying if I said I didn't want to be with you. I've thought about you so much over the past months."

This was exactly what Sarah needed to hear after the way things had gone with Vince but the timing was all wrong. She had work to do here. She couldn't afford to get emotionally involved with anyone right now.

He looked into her eyes and there was a hint of sadness in his. "You never even left me your number. Was it so bad?"

"No, Angelo, it was wonderful." Sarah remembered how tender, generous and thorough Angelo had been as a lover and her body tingled, reminding her how much she enjoyed that night. "It was everything I needed at the time. Honestly, I didn't have a number to give. I was in training."

A shadow crossed Angelo's face. "So I was an *exercise*?"

Don't offend the man, Sarah. He's rich, he's a professional and so handsome.

"No! No, of course not."

Well maybe.

She felt her cheeks warming.

How do I tap dance my way around the "rebound guy" conversation?

She tried to explain. "I thought it was just one night."

"It was. It was meant to be just one night, but I couldn't stop thinking of you and wondering where you disappeared to."

"I'm sorry. I would have enjoyed dinner with you. At least now you know it wasn't personal."

"Yes. I also know fate answered my prayers and brought us together again. I won't waste this opportunity like I did the last."

Sarah took a deep breath.

His eyes were determined. He wasn't kidding and he wasn't just flirting.

Sarah saw he meant every word and it sent a warm wave through her to hear a man, any man, talk to her so honestly and passionately.

Eight

Sarah lay in the soft bed, surrounded by luxury. The gauzy curtains ebbed and flowed in the moonlight as the ocean waves lapped against the shore outside. Her mind wandered, as it always did, to Vince.

Why was he so hot one minute and cold the next? Which represented his true feelings? Then it came to her. It was easier for Vince to command her if she were hooked on him.

If he has an emotional hold on me then he can get me to do whatever he wants while continuing to stay loyal. Isn't that my MO? They know about my history with men. Surely, he's seen my psychological profile. I'm just being played again and it is all just part of the job description for him.

~~~

Sarah enjoyed the therapy of cutting vegetables for a salad. All the frustration she felt with Vince could be expressed without anyone being the wiser. She pounded away at a cucumber, creating perfect half-inch slices.

"Still pretty handy with a knife."

She was so engrossed in her own thoughts that the sound of Vince's voice startled her and she dropped her knife onto the floor. Vince picked up the knife and handed it to her, handle first. A twinge of bitterness came through in her voice before she could check herself. "You sure you want to give me one of these?"

Vince looked at her with those soft brown eyes she so loved.

The eyes of a player.

"I trust you."

"Maybe you shouldn't."

He moved closer and touched her chin, turning her face to his. "I do."

Sarah felt herself being drawn toward him. He had his own gravitational pull on her and she found it difficult to resist. His breath was warm on her cheek. His lips were so close.

Her head asked how she could be so angry with him, knowing he was just playing her, and still fall for it. But her heart felt his pull and overruled all logic.

Angelo started talking from down the hall. "Sarah, if Vincenzo doesn't have anything for you to do this afternoon…" He stopped when he saw Vince leaning against the refrigerator. "Ah, Vincenzo, if you have nothing planned for Sarah this afternoon, I thought I would take her for a ride along the coast."

"Sarah's free to do whatever she likes until we get the call from Victor. Then she's on company time."

So damned cool, like he doesn't even care that Angelo is interested in me.

Sarah wanted to see something from Vince, some kind of reaction. But he just walked out of the room without even changing the "I don't give a damn" expression on his face.

He was about to kiss me. He went from hot to cold in a split second. Is this all part of the act? Just to play me so I'll do his bidding? Two can play at that game. I'll make him feel it.

Nine

Vince watched Angelo.

So confident and sure of himself.

On paper, he was a great guy. Maybe even the kind of guy Vince could hang out with and have a few drinks. Only one thing made Vince hate him. He'd been with Sarah. Vince made his best effort to remain civil while the guy showed him around his huge estate.

Pool, check.

Asshole.

Poolhouse. Soft chairs on the patio.

I hate this guy.

Stables converted to a garage holding one Ferrari, one Mercedes sedan and one Ducati motorcycle.

Dick.

Formal gardens, kitchen garden, olive groves. Check.

Big deal.

Gardener comes tomorrow, then not for a week.

Good.

Two domestics. Maid and cook. Both have secret clearances.

Pretentious prig.

"Here is the chapel where you may set up your equipment."

"A chapel?"

Is he serious?

"Yes, it was built in the 1500's. The walls are three feet thick and solid brick."

Vince ran his hand over the virtually indestructible wall as he walked through the solid oak door. "This isn't a chapel, it's a bunker."

"Yes, it has survived many wars. I think you'll find it suitable. I've had electricity installed. Outlet clusters are there and there to minimize drilling."

He pointed to opposite sides of the chapel. "The fireplace has been bricked in and the chimney filled with concrete. Solid oak doors are at either end. It is completely secure."

Vince looked up at the sweeping brick arches that held up the brick roof. "Yeah, this will work just fine."

I've got to hand it to the guy. He has the security bases covered.

"Good. Let's go back to the house. I want to show you my office."

Angelo led Vince back to the house and into a spacious, first floor office, complete with a four by six foot desk, fireplace, floor to ceiling shelves filled with leather bound books, and a sitting area in front of a large picture window.

Two club chairs sat at angles to an antique globe. Angelo walked to the globe and lifted the top to reveal a fully stocked bar. "Discussions among men should always be punctuated with fine liquor. It is the only way to handle important matters. What would you like?"

You got class. I still don't like you.

"Is that Johnny Walker blue?"

Angelo grinned. "My choice as well." He poured the amber liquor into two crystal glasses and handed one to Vince. "Please." He motioned for Vince to sit in one of the chairs.

Gracious bastard. God, I hate this guy.

Angelo sat in the empty chair and smiled at Vince. "Let's be honest, shall we?"

Vince nodded. "Fewer stories to keep straight."

"Are you and Sarah together?"

Vince shifted in his seat. "We work together. What made you ask that?"

"I've been studying people for thirty years, Vincenzo. You obviously don't like me. I've read your dossier. Your mother is Italian so an aversion to Italians is out of the question. My record is impeccable so the only possible reason for you to dislike me as you do is my brief but significant history with Sarah."

Vince didn't break eye contact as he took a drink, savored it and swallowed. "I'd hardly call it significant. What's your point?"

"Obviously I would like to keep our relationship professional but my intentions lie elsewhere with Sarah."

The hair on the back of Vince's neck stood up. "And just what would those intentions be?"

Angelo smiled.

Cocky son of a bitch.

Vince didn't let Angelo speak. "If you're the professional your people make you out to be, I shouldn't have to tell you, as a vital member of my team, Sarah should be allowed to concentrate on the mission at hand rather than fending off advances by our host nation liaison."

"She may not choose to fight them off." Angelo smiled a wide toothy grin. "So you aren't together?"

Back off.

Vince took the last gulp of his drink and stood. "Thanks for the drink, but I need to get my team set up."

Angelo sat back in his chair. "*Prego*, Vincenzo."

~~~

Vince stomped out to the patio and looked at his team enjoying the breakfast Angelo's cook laid out for them. There was fresh squeezed orange juice, espresso and warm, freshly baked pastries.

Sarah appeared completely at home with an espresso in her hand and a smile on her face.

What a beautiful smile.

When her gaze met his, she set her cup down and replaced the smile with a sour look.

I miss that smile. Hey, if she's gonna hold a grudge because I saved her from one of the bad guys then maybe Angelo deserves her.

"Alright people, this isn't a Tuscan vacation. Let's get to work." Vince heard the clink of cups and glasses as his team scrambled behind him. He walked directly to the chapel and started talking. "Our host has graciously granted us the use of this chapel for our base of operations."

"Holy shit, these walls are solid." Jason was doing his job and checking all the walls for vulnerabilities. "This is a damned bunker!"

"Yeah, it'll do. Jason, you set up the armory. Brian, get some security working. Chris, get the communications uplink operational and check in with our handler at Sixth Fleet. Will, we're gonna need the maps and schematics set up and can you check on that shipment from Nikolai to see if it got in yet?"

"What can I do?" Sarah's voice came softly from behind him.

Vince didn't turn around. He didn't want the distraction of thinking about her. "Study that dossier on Victor, and, when Chris is done here, you two can practice your Russian."

A mumble was all he heard in response. "Yes, sir."

~~~

Sarah walked up to her room and pulled Victor's dossier out of her bag. She mumbled to herself over her frustration with Vince. "Study the dossier. Practice your Russian. He might as well have told me to go fuck myself." She dropped the dossier on the bed and changed into her bathing suit. "You want to treat me like an amateur, fine." She grabbed the dossier and her tanning lotion before leaving the room. When she arrived at the patio, still pissed, she mumbled to herself some more as she applied the tanning lotion. "You want to treat me like a bimbo, that's fine, pig."

Sarah browsed through the dossier she could already recite word for word and then dropped it on the table.

"Is that how you study?" Sarah could make out Chris' dimples at ten yards. He was smiling as he asked the question.

Sarah put on a stern look. "No lip from you, Christopher. You know damned well I've already memorized the contents of that file."

He chuckled and continued in Russian. "I know. I know."

Sarah enjoyed their language games. They'd often switch between Russian, French or Spanish, sometimes all three, in the same conversation.

Chris was so easy to talk to their language practice hardly seemed like work at all.

"Don't sweat the boss. He's just feeling a little pressure on this job. The Italians want details, the Agency wants to keep everything quiet and Vince is caught in the middle trying to negotiate between two intelligence agencies while running an operation. It just makes for high tension."

"Yeah, tell me about it."

They continued their conversation in Russian and talked about the weather, golf and whatever else came to mind until Angelo came outside and took a seat near Sarah.

"May I join you?" To Sarah's surprise, he spoke in Russian.

"Of course. I didn't know you spoke Russian."

Angelo's smile lit up his face and the lines at the corners of his eyes punctuated his smile. "There are many things we don't know about each other.

I'd like to change that."

Chris stood. "I think I'll go check the satellite equipment and make sure Jason isn't surfing porn on my computer. Angelo, make sure she gets plenty of practice. Her Russian is coming along but it would do her good to practice with somebody else."

Angelo nodded. "Yes, we'll practice Russian all afternoon." He looked at Sarah. "Go get dressed. We're going for a ride."

"But I have to practice."

"We will practice." He switched easily to Russian. "Now go get dressed."

Sarah was game for anything that removed her from Vince's orbit for a while. A drive with Angelo was just the ticket. She walked quickly to her room and put on shorts and a shirt over her bathing suit. When she returned downstairs, Angelo was waiting in the entryway with two helmets.

She took the helmet he offered. "A motorcycle ride?"

"Yes. It is a beautiful day for it. We can take a ride along the coast. I know a great place where we can have dinner."

"Dinner? Well, maybe I should change."

"No, *cara*. You would be beautiful in kitchen rags." He grabbed her hand. "Let's go." He led her outside to where his Ducati motorcycle waited.

This guy doesn't skimp on anything. Everything he does oozes class.

Sarah put on her helmet and climbed on the bike behind Angelo. She wrapped her arms around him, grateful for the fun distraction he provided at just the right time. If given time to stew alone, she'd have worked herself into a full-blown tizzy over how Vince was treating her. Now, she hadn't a care.

Ten

Sarah and Angelo returned from dinner happy and relaxed after a beautiful sunset ride. It was late when they joined the rest of the team out having drinks on the patio. Angelo excused himself after a few minutes to make some phone calls.

"Hey, pork chop, while Angelo's out of earshot, I think it is time we talked about something important."

Sarah was suddenly aware that all eyes were on her.

This must be serious.

"What is it, Will?"

Will leaned forward in his chair. "It's no secret we're in a pretty risky business here. Something you need but the agency won't tell you about is a fallback plan."

"What do you mean?"

"Well, there are the basics like an alias and a passport to go with it."

"Why would I need that?"

"There are lots of scenarios where you might need to travel undetected by the government. The next thing you need to think about is a place to fall back to."

"But I've got my apartment in Vegas."

"But the agency knows about it."

What Will was saying finally hit. If something, anything, ever went wrong with the agency and her identity was compromised, she'd need to get the hell out of Dodge to a safe haven. "Wow." She blinked hard a couple of times while the necessity of such a plan struck home. "I really never thought of that." She looked around the small patio at the other guys. "Do you guys all have plans?"

Will spoke up first. "I've got a horse property in Venezuela."

Brian smiled. "You know about my place in Mexico."

"I've got some isolated property in northern Montana." Jason put his feet up on an empty chair. "Good hunting up there."

Sarah looked at Chris and smiled. "Let me guess. Something on a golf course?"

Chris grinned and put on his best Scottish accent. "Near St. Andrews in Scotland."

Sarah pulled her gold cigarette case from her pocket and lit a cigarette.

"What about you, Vince?"

Vince nodded. "I've got a place in Dubai."

Will stood and stretched. "Give it some thought, kid. You never know when you might need that fallback plan. When you work it out, let me know. I've got a good guy who can do up some identity documents for you." He yawned. "Goodnight, ladies."

Chris yawned. "Yeah, I'm calling it a night."

"Me, too." Jason laid his hand on Sarah's knee. "For you, I'm thinking Monaco."

"Not a bad idea." Brian stretched. "Night, darlin'."

Sarah watched as all but Vince walked into the house, suddenly uncomfortably aware they were alone together.

The tip of his cigarette glowed brightly as he took a drag in the dark.

"He's got a point there. Monaco is good. You speak the language. No taxes and people don't ask about each other's pasts because they all have something to hide. Good place to disappear while still keeping a semblance of a life."

Sarah knew he was right but just didn't want to admit it.

Why does it bother me so much that he's with other women? We can't be together. I have no right to be jealous. It's not like I couldn't find a man of my own. Hell, Angelo is single and a great way to pass some time.

"I'll figure something out." Sarah stood as her body crawled with discomfort. She hated that being alone with him hurt so much. "I'm going to hit the hay too. Goodnight." She walked quickly into the house. The light was on in Angelo's study, and she poked her head in the door. "*Buona notte*, Angelo."

He looked up from his computer. "Going to bed so early? Please, come in. Will you join me in a drink?"

"Sure. That would be nice. Thank you."

Sarah walked into the study and was surprised at what a comfortable room it was. She sat in one of the large leather chairs by the huge globe and watched as Angelo poured a glass of Brandy.

He gave her the glass and poured one for himself. "*Salut.*"

Sarah raised her glass. "*Salut.*"

Angelo sat in the other leather chair and sighed. "So how did you come to be in this business, Sarah?"

Sarah sat back and took a deep breath. "Long story."

"I have all night."

"I'd had a very bad day." She was finally able to smile about the day she was discharged from the Air Force and then found her boyfriend with another man. "I was a cop in the U.S. Air Force, but I was overweight so they discharged me."

"Overweight? That is ridiculous."

Sarah smiled at the handsome Italian. "I didn't always look like this, Angelo."

He raised his eyebrows in interest. "Continue, please."

"My commander gave me a business card for a camp where I could lose weight. It was all very secretive. I called, they accepted me and I lost weight. As it turned out, it was a training camp for the C.I.A." She chuckled. "After being tested, I was asked to join this team. I accepted."

"But why? Surely you must have had other options?"

"Not really. I had no idea what I was going to do. I loved being a military cop but couldn't see myself in a civilian police force."

Angelo nodded.

"I liked the idea of being in a form of law enforcement that got results every time we went out on an operation. I still like it. I also liked the security the job gave me. I take risks but I earn a good living and that is something I've never had. I've always lived from paycheck to paycheck and never had any form of financial security. I've even been homeless more than once."

Angelo seemed surprised.

"Now I have some security. I have a small luxury apartment at the MGM Grand in Las Vegas and a new Jeep to get around town. They aren't much but they are paid for. They're mine. I live simply and invest my paycheck."

"But how can you date with such a life?"

"I don't. Men have used me too much, present company excluded. I'm not anxious to be used again. Long-term relationships have always ended badly for me. Now I just use men on behalf of Uncle Sam."

"A life without love seems so sad for a beautiful woman like you, *cara*."

Yeah, it sounds pretty pathetic when I say it out loud.

"So do you ever plan to marry, to have children?"

"If the right man asks me, I'll certainly consider it but they aren t exactly lining up outside my door." Sarah needed to change the subject before she became depressed. "So what about you, Angelo? Why did you choose this life, and why have you stayed with it for so long?"

"My father was in the Carabinieri. He died in the line of duty when I was ten years old. Two years later, my mother died of a broken heart."

"Oh, Angelo, I'm so sorry."

"My sister, God bless her, raised me. She passed away last year. She gave me everything she could while I was growing up but nothing could replace Mama and Papa. When I was young, I was idealistic and wanted to avenge their deaths. I joined the Carabinieri with that in mind. Then I grew up. I saw the evil in the world when I joined the G.I.S."

"You never married?"

"No. I could never put a woman through what happened to my mother. I always thought there would be time for that when I retired." He grinned.

"But you've been at this for thirty years. When will you retire?"

Angelo leaned toward Sarah. "I'll let you in on a little secret. I've already filed the papers. I'll retire after this operation. I've spent too many years fighting. It is time to sleep late, make love, have babies and live the life I've been protecting all these years."

Sarah smiled at how his eyes sparkled when he said those words. No matter what he did, Angelo seemed to be so passionate about life. "And do you have a woman selected to bear your babies?"

He paused. "*Cara*, we are so compatible. We both want a simple life. You would want for nothing here with me. I have worked too long and seen too much to ever take you for granted." He took her hand in his. "I could love you if you let me."

The good guy offering me the good life? There's a switch!

"Oh, Angelo. I don't know what to say."

"I've never met another woman like you, Sarah."

"Oddly enough, and I don't mean to be rude, but I've heard that before."

"I mean it, Sarah."

"I know you do, Angelo."

"Why would you continue with this work?"

"Somebody has to do it."

"Do you really believe that?"

"Yes, I do. I believe what I do is very important."

"Of course, it is, but what about you? What about your own life? Don't you want more?"

"Angelo, the life I had was crap. I gave up that life with pleasure. There was a time when I wanted to settle down with mister right, have a couple of kids and live the American dream, but life happens and you give up silly dreams for reality."

"It doesn't have to be a silly dream. Sarah, how long will you do this?"

"Do what?"

"This job."

"I don't know. Until I can't, or I get a better offer." She smiled.

He took her hand. "Let me make you an offer."

Shock ran through Sarah's body. "What are you saying?"

"Stay with me. Stay here. I'm retiring after this. We could be very happy here. Our children would grow up in a beautiful home, loved and well cared for and you would always be well provided for."

Sounds like a business arrangement.

"Just what are you proposing, a living arrangement?"

"No, marriage, of course."

Affection for this sweet man tugged at her heart but passion wasn't the driving force behind this idea. "But you don't love me. Angelo, you don't even know me."

"I know all I need to know. I know I could love you. What's not to love? Love will grow with time."

I respect you. I enjoy your company. You're great in bed, but I don't love you.

55

"Angelo, I don't…"

"Shh." He put a finger to her lips. "Don't answer now. Think about it. Give me your answer when this mission is over." He stood. "I have an early meeting tomorrow. Please stay and finish your drink."

So considerate.

"Goodnight, Angelo."

He bent and kissed her softly on the cheek. "Goodnight, *cara*."

Sarah considered Angelo's proposition. It was great on paper. He was a great looking guy, older, more mature, knew what he wanted. He had a beautiful home on a huge estate. Any woman would be a fool to turn him down.

I'm a fool. I just can't give up on Vince. I know there is something there, and I'll never forgive myself if I don't give it a chance. I need to know before I move on. Damn. Despite what my head tells me, my heart is still making my decisions.

Eleven

Vince crossed his arms over his massive chest. They rose and fell with every breath he took. "Angelo was kind enough to inform me today that he has proposed to you and you did not say 'no'."

Sarah's face grew hot. She looked around at her teammates and saw expectant looks on their faces. They wanted something.

Surely, they don't think I'll take him up on the offer?

Vince tightened his arms over his chest and scowled at Sarah as though he were waiting for an explanation.

I'm not his damned possession. Where does he get off putting me on the spot in front of the guys like this?

"What the hell is this, an intervention?"

Vince's eyes narrowed. "We'd like some answers."

"To what questions? You've got me cornered here but nobody's asked one question yet."

"We want to know when you were planning on telling us."

"Telling you what?"

"That you're thinking about quitting."

"Oh, and every time one of you thinks about retirement, you get all touchy-feely and tell everyone about it? Give me a break!"

"This is different. If we're planting you undercover, we need to know where your loyalties lie."

"My loyalties? *My* loyalties!" Sarah jumped out of her chair and pointed at Vince. "I pulled your unconscious body off a fucking time bomb and you have the balls to question my loyalty? How dare you!"

Vince roared. "Hey, we talked about a backup plan, but we didn't mean marry the first guy who asks you! I understand things change. We all do. We just think you should let us know when those changes affect us."

So that's it. He can have his but as soon as I get an offer, my loyalty is questioned.

"Yeah, things change alright. Sometimes things change quicker than overnight, but you'd know all about that, wouldn't you, Vince?"

"I don't know what is wrong with you."

"Well, you must because you know everything, don't you, Vince? You know what? If you know everything, then you'll already know my answer for Angelo, and my telling you would be redundant. So go fuck yourself."

Will lit a cigar and puffed pensively. "Alright. That's enough. We're not getting anywhere this way." He turned to Vince. "Why don't you just sit this one out?"

Will held his cigar between his index and middle fingers and used it to punctuate what he said. "Now listen, pork chop. Nobody here is going to tell you what to do. Contrary to the leatherneck's current demeanor." He shot Vince a hard look. "And apparent lack of communication skills, we wanted to talk to you about this because we care about you."

Sarah sat on one of the patio chairs and lit a cigarette. "Okay, talk." She avoided any eye contact with Vince.

"Look, kid, first of all, you're a damned fine operator, and I rather like having you on the team. Secondly, and this is my own concern as a friend, we all know your personal history of bad relationships with men prior to the Camp picking you up. I'd hate to see you fall back into that."

Sarah tapped an ash into the ashtray on the table beside her. "Thank you, Will. Noted."

Brian squatted on the patio, laced his fingers together and leaned on his elbows, resting on his knees. "I'll admit to being totally selfish here. It normally takes a long time for a team like ours to gel. I saw it with the SEAL teams. We've got a good thing here, darlin', and I'd hate to lose it. Oh, and I might miss you a little."

Sarah smiled at Brian and gave him a slight nod. "Noted."

Chris jumped in. "It is totally your decision, and I never stand in the way of true love, but it takes ten years to break in a good agent. But, like Will and Brian said, you were exceptional at adapting. On a personal note, your golf game is coming along very well, and I've grown accustomed to your company."

Jason stood from his chair and smashed his cigarette into the ashtray on the table. "You guys are a bunch of pussies. I've never been anything but straight with you, girl, so I won't change my approach now." He looked Sarah straight in the eyes from about one foot away. "I don't like Italian guys and this chump ain't any different. He wants a trophy for his retirement. You deserve better than that. You want to be somebody's trophy? I don't think I'm stretching the truth when I say any fucking one of us would be happy as hell to put you on our mantle. Besides, I have yet to meet a chick who can bar crawl like you can. I'd miss you like crazy, and I'd try really frigging hard not to forgive you."

Brian chimed in with a flash of a smile. "Yeah, Jason would never find another hottie to be seen with, much less get into the good clubs without you."

Jason nodded. "True that."

Sarah chain lit another cigarette.

I think they like me. Well, all but him.

Sarah caught Vince staring at her and glared back.

They really think I'm seriously considering this. Why is he pissed?

"Look, I appreciate your input guys. I'm not bailing on this mission. I told Angelo I couldn't give him an answer until we've finished this. I'll keep you in the loop."

"Good enough." Will stood. "Boys?"

Finally, they all walked back to the house. All but one. Vince's brown eyes watched her as she continued smoking her cigarette.

They sat in silence.

God, but you infuriate me!

Vince's voice came rough and ragged through the silence. "Are you seriously considering this?"

Sarah snuffed out her cigarette and stood. "What if I am?"

"You'd be making a big mistake."

"Who are you to tell me what's a mistake?"

Vince stood. "He doesn't love you."

Sarah stood and glared at Vince. "Who does? And so what? What do you know about love? Men who don't love me have been using me all my life. Hell, even you strung me along just so I'd fall in line and play the game."

It was all just a game to him. He knew if he strung me along, I'd do whatever he asked.

Vince grabbed her shoulders and spun her around. "That isn't true. I never strung you along."

Why couldn't it be you offering me love instead of Angelo?

59

Sarah's heart ached and she winced as she pushed free of Vince's grip and resumed her pacing. "Yeah, you did. All it took was two kisses and a string of pearls. Well, I may have been easy but I've had the pearls appraised and can sleep at night knowing at least I wasn't cheap. I hope you put them on your expense account."

"You bitch! You were the one doing the stringing. And here I thought…" He didn't finish.

"Oh, I'm a bitch now? That's rich. You thought what? I'd just do what I'm told and not have a social life while you and the boys go out and get a piece of tail whenever you like? That double standard of yours is bullshit, Vince."

"What double standard? You know, Sarah, my sister is a big fan of your spunk but, quite frankly, I'm frigging tired of it." Vince turned and walked back toward the house. "You do whatever the hell you want.'

Sarah mumbled to no one at all. "Fuck you."

What sister?

Twelve

Sarah rose early and put on her bathing suit for a swim. She walked down to the pool and started doing her laps.

"Ooh, baby! Lookin' good in the thong! You got a little sugar for Big Daddy?"

Sarah looked up and smiled at Chris who just sat down with a cup of coffee. "Good morning." When she realized Vince was sitting at the patio table watching her, she greeted him as well. "Morning, major."

Vince grunted. "Morning."

Chris changed over to Russian without skipping a beat. "I'm telling you, the man has got it bad for you."

Sarah turned to do a backstroke and answered in Russian. "Piss off."

"Come on, when are you guys gonna stop denying the sexual tension between you, get it on and just get it over with? We all know it's gonna happen. And if it happens before our next mission, I get four thousand bucks."

"Nope. Not worth the hassle. Not even for fifty percent of the take."

"Has anybody ever told you it's rude to talk behind people's backs?" Vince opened his newspaper.

Chris answered in English. "We're not doing it behind your back, we're doing it right in front of you, just in another language."

"That's even worse." Vince turned a page.

Chris switched back to Russian. "Seriously, babe. He's mad about you."

"I don't think so, Chris. He's got all the women he can handle already.

Besides, he knows what I do for a living. He's not dumb enough to fall for somebody like me."

"What the hell are you talking about? You're a catch no matter what you do for a living! I'd take you home to meet my mother in a heartbeat. Just say the word." He pulled out his cell phone. "I'll call her right now."

"That's sweet, but that whole happily ever after thing isn't gonna happen for me." Sarah climbed out of the pool and dried off.

"That's just stupid. You know what your problem is? Inside that hottie body is a fat girl's brain. The world is at your feet, girl. You just can't see it because that fat girl's still doing all your thinking."

"I don't mean to be rude, Chris, but I think I'll go take a walk to clear my head." Sarah put on her sunglasses and slipped on her sandals preparing to walk away.

"Be careful out there."

"Yeah, those olive trees are really dangerous." Sarah gave Chris a wink and a smile before turning to go.

Sarah stepped out the front door just as Brian pulled up in a new Maserati Spyder convertible.

A bright smile lit up his face. "Hey, baby! Wanna go get some breakfast?"

"Where did you get a sweet set of wheels like this?"

"Perks of the job. We need a car to get to the meeting. Can't have an international arms dealer showing up in a Honda Civic."

Sarah walked around to the passenger side, trailing her fingers in a gentle caress over the purring sports car. "Nice."

"Come on, darlin! Let's take it for a spin. It needs a beautiful woman in the passenger seat. Get in before Jason spots us. If I take him for a ride, everyone will think I'm gay."

"I don't know, Brian. Jason will be pissed if he misses out on this."

"Come on, Sarah. I need to find me some Italian tail." He lowered his sunglasses and raised his eyebrows. "You can be my wingman."

Sarah opened the door and hopped in. "Well, since you put it that way."

Thirteen

Sarah walked out to the patio with a cup of coffee in her hand. Her outing with Brian the day before had been a bit more than a drive. He insisted on exploring every bar and café on the Genoa coast in his search for an Italian hottie. Sarah found it an excellent opportunity to enjoy an Italian favorite, limoncello. It went down like lemonade, but she was feeling the vodka this morning.

Chris was lying on a chaise, working on his tan. He spoke in Russian.

"Good morning. How are you today?"

"I've been better."

He smiled. "I'm here."

Chris was always there when Sarah needed to talk, true to his word when she first met him as the team's communications specialist and he delivered that corny "I'm here if you want to talk" line.

"Vince mentioned a sister who knew me, but I've never seen her. What do you know about his family?"

"His father is Shawn Hennesee, twenty years enlisted in the Marines then became an agency man. His mother is Italian. They met during a tour he did over here. Siblings are two brothers and a sister. Anthony is in Explosive Ordinance Disposal in the Marines. He's on a tour in Iraq. I've never met him.

Their brother Marco died two years ago serving in Afghanistan. His sister, Regina, was military before she married. She chose to get out when she got pregnant with her first child. Didn't you meet her when she was in town before we left? Good looking woman." Chris raised his eyebrows and turned toward

Sarah. "Don't tell Vince, but I wouldn't throw her out of bed for eating crackers."

Sarah's mind raced. She felt a sudden weight in her stomach and the need to retch.

"Chris?"

"Yeah."

"Is she about my height with long, dark, curly hair?"

"Yep. Spitting image of her mother too."

Oh, shit. I punched Vince out in front of his sister?

Sarah's stomach rolled. "That was his sister?"

"Come to think of it, she was pretty anxious to meet you."

The depth of her misunderstanding hit her in the face like a bag of pennies.

I think I called her a bimbo, too. And he didn't say anything because he's too frigging proud.

Chris must have seen the look on Sarah's face. "You should talk to him, Sarah, alone. Get this sorted out."

Sarah sprung out of her chair, leaving her coffee behind.

"Thanks for the intel, Chris."

"It's what I do. This and golf are all I've got."

~~~

Sarah burst into the chapel. Vince was the only one there. He spun around, Sig in hand and aimed at Sarah's head.

Sarah raised her hands and stopped in her tracks. "Whoa!"

"Jesus, woman! Can't you ever enter a room without exploding into it?"

He switched the safety on the handgun and tucked it into his waistband.

Sarah dropped her hands slowly. "I think you've just given me the motivation to work on that."

She walked up to him and stopped within arm's reach. "I need to talk to you."

"Is it mission related?"

"No."

He turned away and studied some photos on the table behind him.

"Then we don't need to talk."

"Vince." She paused to swallow her pride and nearly choked on it. "I need to talk to you now."

His shoulders seemed to soften as he turned to face her.

"I'm sorry."

"What did you do now?"

"All of it."

"I don't know what you're talking about, woman."

"I didn't know he was an arms dealer. I didn't know she was your sister. I thought…"

Oh, hell. This is going to be hard.

"You thought what?"

He's going to make me say it.

Sarah swallowed the bitter pill and spoke quickly to get it out before she chickened out. "I thought it was personal and you didn't want me to date while you did. I didn't know she was your sister, and I was jealous. Okay, there it is. I'm sorry."

Sarah swallowed the frog that nearly choked her during her apology and turned to go before the tear welling up decided to drop.

Vince's strong hands landed on her shoulders and she stopped. She swallowed hard as the tear rolled.

Vince wrapped his arms around her and she melted into him when she felt his breath on her neck.

Vince sighed. "Damn you, woman."

Sarah turned around and looked into his soft brown eyes. "I'm so sorry."

He smiled. "There hasn't been room in my life for any other woman since you exploded into it."

Sarah swallowed another tear and hugged Vince.

I don't want to let go.

"I think about retirement all the time, Sarah." One hand held her close to him while the other enmeshed itself in her hair and gently cupped the back of her head. "I've been thinking about it ever since I first saw you."

Sarah looked into his eyes. "I didn't mean what I said. I love the pearls. I do."

Vince's lips were within a breath of hers. He smiled and cut her off mid sentence with a whisper. "Shut up."

His lips touched hers. Gently, softly, lovingly. He pulled her close.

Sarah's heart beat hard and fast. She gasped for breath but didn't want the kiss to end. Her fingertips tingled as she ran them over his shoulders. Her body ached for him, and she embraced the moment.

It may be all we have.

Vince's phone rang and the moment was gone.

He looked into her eyes and apologized with a whisper. "I'm sorry. I have to take this."

She took a step back.

He opened the phone. "Hennessee."

"Victor. Good to hear from you." Vince stepped back, but his eyes never left Sarah's. "Tonight is just fine. Yes, I do know the place." He grinned. "No, that won't be necessary. I've got one. Yeah, this one's more than enough. Okay, we'll see you then." Vince closed his phone and slid it into his pocket. "We're on tonight."

Sarah was curious about the strange conversation. "What did he ask you?"

A devious smile spanned Vince's face. "If I needed a female guest for my entertainment."

"He didn't ask in quite those words, did he?"

"Nope." Vince winked at Sarah. "Now get Jason to drive you into Milan.

He's been itching to drive that Spyder. Go buy yourself something slutty. You and I are going out for drinks and dancing tonight."

Sarah turned to leave and spoke over her shoulder as she walked away. "I should probably be offended by those instructions, but Jason has been saying the same thing to me every Friday since our last mission."

Fourteen

Sarah waited while Vince left the slick, black Maserati with the valet outside the nightclub. She eyed him as he walked toward her. His smooth movements and the black silk suit were a stunning combination.

Damn, those Marines clean up nice.

She didn't break her stare when he checked her out from head to toe. A thrill shot through her when he smiled. She threw her shoulders back and tossed her hair over her shoulder. "Passable?"

He took her arm. "Yeah, I'd definitely make a pass at you."

She smiled and raised an eyebrow. "Well, what are you waiting for?"

"We're on the job. Business first, then pleasure, Sarah."

Sarah grabbed Vince by the lapels and kissed him hard.

He enveloped her in his arms and returned the kiss with gusto.

When he released her, she took a deep breath and willed her body to calm down. "And what a pleasure it will be. I'll be here all night, unless I get a better offer."

He beamed at her as though he were about to say something but thought better of it. Vince tipped the doorman and said something Sarah couldn't hear over the sound of the music. The doorman nodded and motioned to a man inside who led them into a VIP room upstairs.

Vince appeared ever the gentleman. He offered Sarah his arm as they climbed the stairs and she followed his lead.

Hard to believe he was once a U.S. Marine. Well, maybe not so hard.

As they reached the second floor landing overlooking the dance floor, Sarah had her first good look at the real, live Victor Bolshoi.

He lounged on a banquette, leaning back, as a shapely redhead straddled his right thigh and ran her hands under his silk jacket. He smiled as she nibbled on his ear.

About ten feet away was a small dance floor, overlooking the club's main dance floor below, where three other women danced together. None of them seemed significant to Victor. The only woman who held his attention was the redhead.

The man who led Sarah and Vince upstairs cleared his throat.

Victor's brown eyes opened and he pushed the redhead off him with his left hand, which fairly spanned her entire right buttock. He lifted an eyebrow at Sarah.

The Ukrainian stood from his seat and smiled. He was tall, maybe six-foot-three. His hair was brown and short, but long enough to tousle if you liked to do that sort of thing. His features were strong and blocky very *Ivan Drago*, only a bit more color with the brown hair and eyes. All in all, Sarah had to admit, he wasn't ugly.

Isn't it amazing how the big time criminals take such good care of themselves?

Knowing he had a thing for coke, Sarah was surprised at how fit the man was. He wore a tight tee shirt under his designer jacket and there was definitely muscle under there. Sarah sized up the abs and blocky chest and looked for some sign of how much thigh he might have.

This guy looks way too muscular to mess with hand to hand. Let's see if the charm works.

"Mr. Hennessee!" He reached out to shake Vince's hand.

Vince reciprocated. "Please, call me Vince."

Victor eyed Sarah. "While it is customary to bring a gift, I must say you've outdone yourself."

Vince put his arm around Sarah's shoulders. "Ah, this one is mine tonight but, hey, anything can happen. Right, baby?"

Sarah was still riding the wave of longing the kiss outside inspired. "Oh, yeah."

Victor responded in Russian to Vince. "Let me know when you're done with her. I'd tap that."

Sarah tried not to cringe as she pretended not to understand Russian.

Money can't buy you class.

Vince replied in kind. "What? This old thing? Just a little something I threw on."

He speaks Russian? Holy crap, he understood that whole conversation between me and Chris!

Victor laughed a hearty belly laugh and ushered Vince to the table.

Sarah followed dutifully like the bimbo she was supposed to be.

Vince put his hand on her knee as she sat. "Why don't you go powder your nose, sweetheart?"

Sarah stood and strutted past the two Russian henchmen and through the door to the ladies room.

He speaks Russian? What the hell am I here for?

Sarah opened her tiny crystal encrusted purse and removed her lipstick. When she looked into the mirror to apply it she saw something she might never get used to. The fat girl she always expected wasn't there. In her place was a knockout staring back at her. A smile curled her lips. After recovering from her initial shock, she got her head back into the game.

This old thing isn't looking so bad just yet. Guess you'll have to suffer through it, Hennessee.

Vince and Victor didn't seem to discuss business at all over the course of the evening. If they did, it was while Sarah was in the ladies room. She hated being left out of the details but that wasn't her part. It might have been easier for her if she'd had a part in the dealing, logistics or planning. Instead, she had to pretend to be everything she wasn't— flighty, superficial and unintelligent. In a way, it was a relief to get away from herself. She was beginning to think she might be too steady, too deep and way too smart for her own good.

Just think how easy life would be if I were only a dumb bimbo.

Vince was particularly attentive and she took every advantage of his act.

Just because you don't get to go home with the actor doesn't mean you can't enjoy the show.

Vince's efforts seemed to be paying off with Victor. When Vince ran his hand along Sarah's barely covered, toned and tan thigh, Victor watched with heavy breaths. When Vince nuzzled her neck and whispered in her ear, Sarah leaned in and let her fingers do the walking under his jacket and into his shirt so the whole room knew she was enjoying every minute of it. It didn't hurt that it seemed to encourage Vince to continue.

Oh, yeah.

After a few drinks, Victor called to one of the women who was putting on a seductive performance for him and excused himself to join her on the small dance floor in the VIP lounge.

Vince stood. "Come on, baby. Time to dance for your dinner." He wrapped his arm around Sarah's waist as she stood and escorted her onto the dance floor near Victor.

He pulled her so close that Sarah had to take a breath to remember where she was. Vince led her perfectly with one hand in hers and the other at the small of her back. Her heart matched time with the quick Latin beat and she let Vince carry her away to some place she'd never been.

She was no longer the timid girl who'd given in to a gay man's plan, nor was she the bold broad who wasn't afraid of taking on four muggers on the street. She was somebody else entirely. She was warm, passionate, desperately in love and scared shitless of all that entailed.

Vince moved like a cat.

Sarah barely knew she was being led. A rush of excitement surged through her as she became suddenly aware of his hips leading her, his thighs against hers and his chest firm and muscular against hers. They'd been dancing around each other at work and avoiding their obvious chemistry for so long that finally being in such intimate proximity and moving together was about as close to foreplay as Sarah could imagine.

"Do all Devil Dogs dance this well?"

"Only the ones whose sisters forced them to be their dance partners."

Sarah grinned. "I find it hard to believe anyone could force you to do anything you didn't want to do."

He shook his head. "You'd be surprised at what a good woman can make a man do when she puts her mind to it."

"Oh, really?"

"Yeah." He pulled her even closer. "You should try it sometime."

The song ended.

Sarah swallowed hard as she thought about what his statement might imply. "I might just do that."

Vince wrapped both arms around her and held her there a moment longer.

His eyes gleamed and Sarah allowed herself to look into them. She ached to tell him with her eyes what she could never say out loud.

There's the devil in those eyes, but I will love them until I die.

She felt his breath on her cheek and his chest rising and falling quickly against her own. The music, the people and even the room disappeared. When his lips touched hers, every nerve in her body exploded with excitement.

Take me now.

Vince released her all too soon.

When Sarah opened her eyes, the real world and their mission returned to her mind.

Victor smiled suggestively and Sarah hoped it meant he was ready to take the bait.

The more you want me, the more mistakes you'll make. Let's get this mission done.

~~~

"Honey, why don't you go hang out with the girls while we talk business?" Vince watched Sarah for a moment as she walked over to the small group of women, who were Victor's entourage, and began dancing with them.

Victor watched her too. "She's exquisite. Where did you find her?"

Vince turned and they both walked back to the table. "I picked her up at a party in Milan."

"Oh, really?" Victor sat and poured them both more scotch. "Do you plan on keeping her long?"

Vince looked into the man's eyes and lied without blinking. "I'm just having some fun while I'm in Italy. Why? You interested?"

He nodded. "I might be. I might be." He smiled as he took a drink.

Vince gazed at Sarah and took a deep breath as he drank her in. He admired how Sarah didn't miss a beat and started dancing seductively with a redhead who had legs up to her neck. Sarah seemed to know exactly what to do to get a guy on the hook.

Victor was practically drooling.

Vince glanced at Victor. "I could put in a good word for you."

Victor didn't take his eyes off Sarah while he spoke. "I'll take one hundred thousand off the price if you throw her in."

Vince knew by the look on the guy's face he could get more than that for her, but he had to pay something for the gunship or he couldn't make the bust.

71

Vince took a drink of his Scotch and gave Victor a single, slow nod. "I'll ask her in the morning, but I may have spoiled her for other men by then." A wry smile curled his lips.

Victor stood and took another look at Sarah. "I'll take my chances." He shook Vince's hand. "Call me tomorrow then. Now, if you'll excuse me, I have some women to spoil, too."

Vince stood and motioned to Sarah.

She sidled up to him.

Is this the act or the real thing? I'll be damned if I can ever read this woman.

Vince decided to take advantage of the act and wrapped his arms around her. She fit perfectly to him.

He bent his head and kissed her hard and deep.

Might as well sell it.

She followed just as he'd hoped. This was one of the few times when he really loved his job.

My God, she smells good enough to eat.

She tasted like limoncello. He wondered what the rest of her tasted like.

If only I really did have you for tonight. Now the show has to end so Victor can think I'm taking you back to a hotel to rock your world, and rock it I would.

He pulled himself from her soft lips and looked into her eyes. They were glazed over.

Had she had that much to drink?

He kept one hand on her waist and walked her out into the cool night air outside the club as she clung to him.

She played her part perfectly, kissing him and pawing his chest under his jacket as they waited for the valet to bring their car. Had she rubbed up against him a little more closely she'd know exactly how much he was enjoying her touch. He opened the car door and watched her slide in to the open-topped convertible.

Lucky seat.

Vince walked around the sports car and stepped in. When he turned the key in the ignition and the engine started to purr, Sarah turned to him. "Do we have to go back yet?"

She likes the car. Good taste.

"Nah, Maseratis don't turn into pumpkins."

She sighed. "Good." She stroked his thigh and let her hand rest there for a moment.

That hand on my thigh is no act. God help me. I have to sell this woman tomorrow, but all I want tonight is to own her.

"So you speak Russian?"

"Fluently. You don't deal arms for five years and not learn Russian."

"Why didn't you tell anyone?"

He powered the Maserati out of the parking lot and into the night traffic.

"Will knows." He couldn't help himself as a grin spread across his face. "He's fluent too in case you want to have private conversations in front of him."

Her eyes opened wide and her mouth dropped open before she composed herself again. Her blood went cold with embarrassment over the conversation she and Chris had at the pool while Vince was reading a newspaper. "Why didn't I know?"

"You didn't ask."

"Does Chris know?"

"No." Vince looked at Sarah quizzically. "You'd think he would if he were doing his job right. I'm going to have to talk to him about that. He thinks that's why we brought you."

"Well then why *did* you bring me?"

"Bait of course. Russian bear. American honey pot." Vince smiled.

"Besides," he fingered the hem of her mini skirt and let his thumb stoke her thigh under the fabric, "it was a great excuse to dress you up and take you out without the boys tagging along."

She sat back in her seat. "You took me to an arms deal." She shook her head. "Damn, Hennessee, you really know how to treat the ladies. What do you do when you really like a girl, take her to Africa for a little civil war?"

He shifted into a lower gear and turned off the main road onto a gravel road leading to the beach. "If you must know, I've got a little island in the United Arab Emirates, but hey, whatever get's you hot. I'm there."

I am so there.

Fifteen

Vince turned off before they reached the road to Angelo's house. Sarah glanced at him as she pulled the earpiece out of her ear and tucked it in her purse. She hoped his hand on her thigh meant they would finally seal this deal and give in to the chemistry they both clearly felt. If it did, she didn't need Chris listening in.

The dirt road wound its way down to an empty beach where Vince parked and shut off the car.

Sarah turned to Vince in the driver's seat. "This is nice. How did you know about it?"

"My mother is from this area. My cousins and I used to come down here when I was a kid." He looked around. "This beach hasn't changed a bit."

"I had no idea you'd spent so much time in Italy. Do you still have family here?"

Vince smiled. "A little. My grandmother, six aunts, five uncles, eighteen cousins and their kids."

Sarah gaped. "A little, huh?"

He got out of the car, took off his shoes, jacket and tie and then walked around to open Sarah's door.

She slipped off her shoes and took the hand he offered as she stepped out of the car. "That's a pretty big family. You must take some heat being single, huh?"

Vince held her hand as they walked toward the incoming tide. "Not as much as you might think. Nonna and the aunts didn't approve of the ex." He glanced sideways at Sarah. "You remember Lori?"

"How could I forget the woman who accused me of trying to steal you, jumped me in an alley and sucker punched me?"

Vince shook his head and chuckled. "You showed her. Anyway, they're still hoping I'll find a good woman, meaning one they approve of, to have lots of kids and settle down with."

"Good luck with that."

"Ah, I don't think it will be too difficult."

"How's that? Be careful you don't trip on your ego while you're thinking of an answer." She nudged him with her shoulder to punctuate the playful dig.

"I figure they'll take to you just fine."

Sarah's face grew hot, and she caught her breath.

Can this really be happening?

"I was thinking we could go have a meal with the family when this is done. We'll have to bring the boys though. They'd never forgive us if we didn't. Besides, Nonna's cooking will soften the blow when I tell them I'm retiring."

Sarah smiled at Vince. "Really?"

Vince stopped walking and pulled Sarah close against his chest. "Yeah.

My brother, Anthony, returned from Iraq yesterday. It isn't personal any more. I'm ready to do some living. What do you say, Sarah? Will you leave the spy game and swing on a hammock with me?"

Sarah's heart leapt. "Absolutely."

No more pretending. I can finally be with Vince!

They held each other as they stood silently watching the sea.

Sarah's heart raced as she closed her eyes and inhaled the sea air mixed with the musky smell of Vince's neck.

Vince was the first to break the silence. "Have you given Angelo your answer?"

Sarah sighed. She didn't want to hurt Angelo. "Not yet. He asked me to give him my answer when the mission is finished."

"Were you going to say yes?"

Sarah looked up at Vince and shook her head as she stroked his shoulders. "It wouldn't have been fair to him when I'm in love with someone else."

Vince pulled her closer and touched her lips with his. "He's got a lot to offer, you know. Money, stability…"

"I don't need those things. I can always get a job as a trainer at the Camp."

"Yeah?"

"Yeah. I've been sparring with students. Young told me he'd hire me if I ever wanted out of the field. I didn't until now."

"Seriously? You wouldn't miss the thrill?"

Sarah shook her head. "Not at all."

"Huh."

"What?"

"He offered me a job too." Vince grinned a wide, perfect smile. "We could carpool."

They both laughed.

A giddiness overtook her. She had a decent nest egg, a great job and a truly good guy who wanted to introduce her to his grandmother. She finally had everything she'd always wanted.

Vince's phone rang. He looked at the caller ID and then answered.

"Yeah, Will? We're fine. We'll be back shortly to debrief." He put the phone back in his pocket and frowned at Sarah.

"We have to go?"

He nodded. "This is our last mission." He ran his hands through her hair and wound them down her neck and arms. "Let's get it done and start doing some living."

"Since you put it that way."

~~~

Sarah looked around the patio at Angelo's house. The night was quiet and the moon lit the pool and patio in soft light. Chris and Brian reclined on chaises while Will and Jason sat at the table.

Vince held a chair for Sarah as she sat. "Victor offered to knock a hundred thousand off the price if I threw Sarah in to the deal. I think we've got him." He took a seat at one of the other chairs at the large patio table.

Will stood, mumbled something and then spoke up. "Tell him, Chris."

Chris looked up at Will. "But I don't…"

"Just tell him anyway."

Chris sat up in the chaise and ran his hand through his hair. Sarah had come to know this small gesture as Chris' tell. The sign that gave away the fact he was nervous about something. "Vince, there's been something in his communications. I can't quite put my finger on it, but I get the impression he isn't the top dog."

Vince's eyes opened wide and he tilted his head slightly. "What? I've been selling guns to low-ifes and bottom dwellers for years only to find out the guy they say is at the top isn't?"

Will sat in his chair. "It's bigger than that, man."

"That's it. We'll buy the chopper, but Sarah is out of the deal"

Sarah leaned forward. "What are you talking about? I'm the best chance we have to identify the top guy."

"No. We're not putting you in the deal without being sure of the situation."

"That's the whole point, Vince. I need to go in and get that information so we *can* be sure."

Jason lit a cigarette and shook his head. "I'm not gettin' a warm fuzzy from any of this."

"Me neither." Brian took a drink from the sapphire blue bottle of water and placed it back on the table next to his chaise.

Chris leaned forward on his elbows. "Can we regroup without compromising you guys?"

"That's what we have to figure out. Why don't you guys go get some rest. Will, Sarah and I are going to talk and then we'll discuss this as a team tomorrow."

Sarah looked at Will. "Why aren't they staying for this?"

Will waited for the guys to enter the house. He motioned for Sarah to remove her earpiece.

She realized it was still in her purse and gave him the all clear. "Because Nikolai doesn't know them."

"But he…"

He's part of the same organization. Oh, shit.

Sarah suddenly felt very unsure of the mission and nervously lit a cigarette.

"Alright." Will sat at the table and lit a cigar. "Let's break this down and see what we have left. Sarah, what do Nikolai and his mother know about you?"

"I'm a student at UNLV studying international business. My aunt left me some money. I live comfortably and travel whenever the urge hits me. That's the only story I use and I never give details."

Vince cleared his throat. "Do they know where you live?"

"No. I never give that information."

"It would be easy enough to get from UNLV though."

"No. I use a post office box for everything."

"Vince, did you tell him you knew Sarah?"

"Negative. Seen her around, but that's it." Vince rubbed his head.

"Victor is the only one who can place Sarah with us. I told him I picked her up in Milan."

Will nodded. "Your story and her story work."

"Yeah but I don't like it when Chris gets feelings he can't put a finger on. Maybe we should do the deal and keep Sarah out of it. I don't want to place her if we're unsure of the situation."

"Vince, I need to be a part of this. You and I both know it. I can get the information that will make the Italians' case stick. Otherwise they'll hold him for a couple days before a very expensive lawyer gets him out on bail and he skips the country to keep on doing what he does."

"Yes, but if we've been compromised and fed a story to set us up, you could get hurt or worse." He placed his hands palm down on the table and shook his head. "No." He looked into Sarah's eyes. "It's too dangerous. I don't want to put you in this operation."

"Vince." Sarah took a deep breath and placed her hand on top of his. "I'll be okay. The flighty, party girl cover will work fine."

"I agree with Sarah. Chris could just be over-cautious. Sarah's participation can make the difference between information and solid evidence. We need that evidence."

Vince sat back in his chair. "Alright, I don't like it but the final decision is up to you, Sarah."

Sarah squeezed his hand and looked into Vince's eyes. She yearned to be done with this assignment so they could just run away together.

I know you won't let anything happen to me.

She looked over at Will. "You guys will have my back?"

Will nodded. "Always."

She nodded. "Let's do it."

Sixteen

The leggy redhead that Sarah had danced with the night before greeted them at the door of Victor's villa. She greeted Sarah with a warm smile and a kiss on each cheek then looked Vince over like he was on the menu. "Good evening. Please come in. Victor has been expecting you." She motioned them into the house and led them into the large main room centered around a huge stone fireplace. The open windows allowed a slight breeze through the room.

The walls were a golden hue, enhanced by the soft lighting from the wall sconces and the honey colored wood floors.

Sarah ran her hand over one of the soft as butter leather sofas and inhaled the heady scent of leather, a touch of smoke and ocean air.

Victor smiled as he sat in one of two large leather chairs and motioned for Vince and Sarah to sit on the sofa. "Sarah, Vince tells me you met in Milan.

How long will you stay in Italy?"

Sarah crossed her legs at the knee and licked her bottom lip for Victor's benefit. "I have a few weeks before I have to be back in Las Vegas."

Victor didn't take his eyes off Sarah. "Carolina, my dear, will you come here, please?"

The buxom redhead in a mini-dress the same color as her hair sauntered over and sat on the arm of Victor's chair with a sublime smile. "Yes, Victor?"

Victor kept his eyes on Sarah. "See if you can convince Sarah to be our guest for a few weeks while I talk business with Mr. Hennessee."

Carolina stood and took Sarah's hand. "It would be my pleasure."

Carolina led Sarah through the kitchen where she grabbed a bottle of wine and two glasses. She held them up for Sarah to see and flashed a devilish smile.

"Let's have a drink and chat."

Sarah followed as Carolina led her through a set of French doors and onto the patio. Uneasiness about this mission nipped at her nerves but, like getting off the helicopter on Hassan's yacht, she smiled and presented the picture of calm.

It was that same self-consciousness that being overweight made her feel. She took a deep breath of the warm night air.

Can I do this? Can I fool them all and pull it off?

Carolina set the bottle and glasses down on the table and took a seat in one of the chairs. She motioned to another chair. "Please, sit. We can talk about important things while they talk business."

"Very nice." Sarah nestled into the soft chair across the table from Carolina as she poured the wine.

Carolina handed her a glass and raised her own. "Yes, it is." She took a drink of the wine and sighed. "It's not a bad deal with Victor. He pays us every week just to be arm candy and entertainment."

"And by entertainment, you mean?"

She shrugged. "We dance for him and lay around the pool mostly. A little sex, which is always very good, but he prefers coke to women."

Sarah couldn't believe her luck. "Really? This sounds like a very nice deal then."

Carolina reached over and ran her hand through Sarah's hair as she drank with the other hand. "I love your hair."

"Thank you. I love your color." Sarah knew the score. Carolina was Victor's gatekeeper. She gave her a flirty smile. "Is it yours?"

"You'll find out soon enough."

They both smiled in agreement and drank.

"Are you staying in a hotel? I'll have Carlo pick up your things."

Thank goodness Jason and I set up that hotel room with my luggage today.

"Who is Carlo?"

"He's the houseman. He does a bit of gardening and takes care of, well, whatever or whoever needs taking care of."

"I see." The domestic picture was beginning to clear up for Sarah. She pulled the hotel key out of her purse and handed it to Carolina. "Room Two-Twenty-Five. The address is on the key. Thank you."

Carolina waved toward the French doors and they opened.

Sarah watched the man who walked toward Carolina. His scuffed boots made hardly a sound as he crossed the patio. He wore a dark blue tee shirt and faded jeans. The tee shirt was tight and showed off muscles that were worked hard. His hair was dark brown and spikey, and he had a few days growth around his jaw line. He took the term ruggedly handsome to new heights. When he reached Carolina, he bent to kiss her on the lips.

Carolina pulled away after a long minute and grinned. "*Tesoro*, this is

Sarah. She'll be staying with us for a while."

He looked Sarah over. "*Incantato, signorina.*"

Sarah's breath caught in her throat when she looked in his eyes. They were the most mesmerizing light blue she'd ever seen. His tan only made them more spellbinding.

How beautiful!

Carolina handed him Sarah's room key. "Room Two-Twenty-Five. Will you be a dear and get her things?"

"*Si.*" He whispered. "I'll put them in the room next to yours."

Sarah watched as he walked back into the house. Apparently, his butt had been worked quite a bit because it looked fantastic in those jeans

Carolina's voice interrupted Sarah's wholly unwholesome thoughts.

"He's exquisite, isn't he?"

Sarah turned back toward Carolina. "Yes, very handsome."

Carolina took a drink of her wine. "He likes you. Your room connects to mine." She licked her lips as she leaned back on one elbow. "You should join us tonight."

They definitely didn't put this in the list of job benefits. It could be an interesting distraction.

Carolina looked through the French doors Carlo had left open. "Oh, it looks like your beefcake is leaving already." She stood. "Shall we go say goodbye?"

Sarah's stomach sank at the words. The last thing she wanted to do right now was work. The scent of roses wafted on the breeze and the waves washing over the beach whispered in the night. She longed to be with Vince.

Instead, she followed Carolina into the villa where they found Vince and Victor shaking hands.

Victor glanced over at the two women and smiled like a cat about to eat two canaries. "Well, Carolina?"

"Carlo is getting her things." She wore a sly grin as she glanced at Sarah. "She'll be staying in the room adjoining mine."

Victor sighed. "Mmm. Perfect." He took Carolina's hand and spoke to Sarah. "We'll be upstairs. Join us when you're done." He and Carolina made it to the first step before he turned around, almost as an afterthought. "Vince, it was a pleasure doing business with you." He gave Carolina's ass a quick slap, she giggled and they walked quickly upstairs.

Sarah and Vince watched as Victor escorted Carolina up the stairs.

When they reached the landing, Vince turned and nodded toward the front door.

Sarah followed him as he stepped out into the warm night.

Vince awkwardly shoved his hands in his pockets and looked down at his shoes. "Will you be alright?"

She leaned in, took a deep breath of his aftershave and exhaled slowly as she looked into his eyes. Those soft, velvety brown eyes that always made her yearn for him. "I'll be fine. Apparently, he prefers coke to women."

Vince shook his head. "What a stupid, stupid man."

Vince reached out and ran his hand along her jaw line and into her hair.

He pulled her swiftly into a kiss, and she gave herself up to him.

Oh, God. This is all I want. I don't give a damn if we end up poor as paupers. I just want you.

When Vince finally pulled away, Sarah shivered and wrapped her arms around herself. The night was warm but she still felt a chill.

Vince's face was stern. "You do everything you have to do to fit in. None of that changes who you are."

Can this guy be for real?

"I've been doing this for a long time, Sarah. It's too dangerous to have moral reservations in this line of work. Do whatever you have to do. Just stay alive."

Sarah smiled and looked into his soft brown eyes one more time. "That, I can do."

The night seemed colder without him pressed against her. She took a deep breath and rubbed her arms as she watched him walk to the sleek, black Maserati.

He gave her one last glance as he buckled his seat belt. "If you call, I'll come running."

Sarah nodded. "I'm counting on it."

The Spyder purred out of the circular driveway and then he was gone.

Sarah took a deep breath, mustered her nerve and walked back into the house. She looked up to see Carlo coming down the stairs.

He spoke with only a slight accent. "May I show you to your room?"

Sarah met him at the bottom of the stairs. "Yes, please."

Sarah followed a few paces behind him, admiring the view.

Damn. That's just nice to look at.

Much as she wanted Vince, she couldn't ignore the fact that this guy was put together nicely. After all, it was her job to notice.

Carlo led her into a small but attractive room with a single bed. Sarah was slightly relieved and allowed a light sigh to escape her lips.

Not likely to be any action here.

Carlo turned to look at her. "Are you tired?"

"Yes, a little. Where is the bathroom?"

Carlo opened the door beside the dresser to reveal an en suite bath. A large double vanity to the left ran the width of the room. To Sarah's right was a large walk in shower encased in clear glass. There was a door at the opposite end of the bathroom.

"Carolina's room?"

"Yes. I'll let you freshen up and relax." Carlo walked through the bathroom door to Carolina's room and closed it behind him.

~~~

Vince walked into the villa and grabbed a bottle of Scotch and a glass on his way through to the patio.

Angelo walked outside as Vince took a seat in the dark and tossed a full glass of Scotch down his throat.

"Where is Sarah?"

"She's with the Ukrainian." Vince poured himself another drink.

"You are an idiot." Angelo spat the words at him.

Vince looked up at Angelo, eyes narrowed to slits. "Excuse me?"

Angelo let rip with a force Vince hadn't yet seen from the normally quiet man. His voice deepened as he roared at Vince. "The way you use her makes me sick." He spread his hands like a man who just didn't understand. "That woman is a beautiful gem who should be adored and you treat her as though she is just another weapon you can toss at those bastards when the ammunition runs out." He stood his ground and glared at Vince.

Vince gulped his second drink, slammed the glass onto the nearby table and stood toe to toe with Angelo. "Look, pal, you may be good at what you do, but we know what we're doing here so just butt out."

Angelo squared his shoulders and seemed ready for a fight. "Do you?

Do you know what you are doing, Vincenzo?"

More than anything, Vince wanted to smash in Angelo's face for telling him off the same way he'd been telling himself off. Going a few rounds with a guy who could take a beating was just what his fragged nerves needed. "Yeah,

I do!"

Make a move. Just make a move.

Angelo shook his head and stretched his arms to emphasize the question. "Why do you fight this war? You are not a child anymore. You don't fight for the sake of fighting. Do you remember why you started fighting in the first place?"

Vince tried to get control of his anger but all he could do was drown it with Scotch. He hated that he'd left Sarah with the Ukrainian. He hated that he was the one putting her in harm's way. He hated himself and all he wanted to do was kill someone right now. Anyone would do. He growled at the other man who loved Sarah, as much out of anger as to stake his claim. "I don't want to talk to you, Angelo."

Angelo leaned closer to Vince's face and snarled back. "Nor I you, but know this—if she returns safely, I intend to do everything in my power to protect her, treasure her and treat her the way she deserves to be treated. I haven't forgotten why I spent nearly thirty years of my life fighting. I fight for love. I fight for the dream of love, the dream of being able to keep those I love safe."

"Whoa, whoa! What the hell is going on out here?" Will shoved his way between Vince and Angelo and gently pushed his hand against Vince's chest to back him up. "I heard you two all the way upstairs."

Vince sat down and poured another drink. "I know we're guests here but if that guy doesn't back off, I'll punch him dead in the face."

Angelo shot Vince a dirty look. "You better hope she comes back safely." He stormed back into the house.

Will pulled up a chair near Vince. "You gonna drink that all by yourself?"

Vince didn't look up from his glass. "That's the plan."

Will shook his head. "You're finished."

Vince drank the amber liquid in his glass and picked up the bottle. "Nope. Got half a bottle left."

"That's not what I'm talking about, man."

"What is it about you guys that makes you think I want to talk?"

"You planted Sarah with the Ukrainian, didn't you?"

"Yep." Vince threw back another glass of Scotch.

"Look, I don't want to get all Doctor Phil on you, man, but it ain't in you to do this anymore. You've lost your edge, and we both know why." Will stood and picked up what was left of the bottle of Scotch. "You don't need this. You need to get your head on so we can bring Sarah back and wrap this up." Will headed back into the house and left Vince alone with nothing but the guilt that haunted him. He had a bad feeling about this operation, and his heart didn't want to hear what his gut was saying.

Seventeen

Sarah woke early and surveyed her surroundings. The room was small but comfortable. A large window overlooked an enclosed garden area. From what she saw, there were walls on three sides of the property that tapered down to nothing as they met the beach. Within the walls were all the amenities one could want. There was a large patio, about ten yards long, leading to the full sized pool and then fifty yards from the pool to the beach. The swimming pool, cascading ponds and the corolla of tropical plants surrounding the main house made it appear to be more of a spa than a fortress. The stone wall surrounding the property stood nine feet high and was topped by three strands of what were probably electrified wires. Several armed guards with machine guns patrolled the grounds.

The sooner we riddle this joint with bullets, the sooner I can go home.

Sarah turned on some music in case Victor had any listening devices in the room. She was so accustomed to wearing the tiny, inserted earpiece she often had to put a finger to her ear to be sure it was still there.

"Chris, are you listening?"

"Good morning, sunshine. Everything alright behind the iron curtain?"

"Yeah, just fine. I have a comfortable bed and a nice view. The only problem is there are three gorgeous women already lounging by the pool. Getting close to Victor won't be easy in this stable of talent."

"Trust me, Sarah. None of those women can hold a candle to you."

"How do you know?"

"Would you believe satellite TV? When you go down there, I'll be able to see you blink."

"No way!"

"You gotta love technology. It takes voyeurism to a whole new level."

"Damn."

"Now wear something skanky for Big Daddy. Have a good day, babe. I'll be here if you need me."

"You too, Chris."

She showered and dressed. The other women wore revealing bathing suits so she chose her white thong bikini to show off her assets. She had the other women as well as Victor's attraction to cocaine to compete with so she steeled herself for a dynamite performance.

Getting Hassan was a cakewalk compared to this job!

Carlo startled her as she stepped outside her room. "Good morning, Sarah."

Sarah turned to see Carlo at Carolina's door. "Good morning, Carlo. Have I missed any fun?"

Carlo walked the last few steps to Sarah and put his arm around her waist in a semi hug. "I think I could bring you up to speed."

Damn. This guy is good.

Sarah smiled, still unsure of Carlo's real role in the household and careful not to burn any bridges. "I'm sure if anyone could, it would be you."

"Victor will be down shortly for breakfast by the pool."

"Thank you, Carlo." Sarah left Carlo in the hallway and walked downstairs to the patio.

A tray with cups, coffee and juice waited on the patio table. As Sarah poured herself a cup of coffee, she felt someone approaching close behind her and took a slow, deep breath.

"Good morning, Sarah. Did you sleep well?"

She turned to see Victor standing behind her in an open, button down shirt and blue jeans. She eased closer to him and fingered his buttons. "Very well, thank you."

"Good. Perhaps tonight we can help you sleep even better?"

Sarah raised an eyebrow and gently stroked Victor's arm. "Sounds intriguing."

Victor reached around her waist. "Good." He whispered in her ear. "That was my intention."

In a moment, he turned to Carolina who was lying by the pool. "Carolina, my dear."

She didn't even look up from where she was lying. "Yes, Victor."

"I think we should go shopping after breakfast. What do you think?"

"Sounds lovely, Victor."

"Carlo, tell the driver we'll be going shopping after I've had my coffee."

"Yes, Victor."

Sarah took a sip of her coffee. "I think I'll go get dressed."

Carolina looked up and smiled. "Let me know if you need any help."

Sarah heard Chris' voice in her earpiece. "I think the redhead has a thing for you."

When Sarah returned to her room to change, Chris explained that she would pick up a "dead drop" during her shopping trip.

A tiny panic overtook her. "Chris, I've never done a dead drop before. I have no idea how to do it."

Brian's voice was the next she heard through the earpiece. "Don't worry, baby. I know I'm your first. I'll be gentle. Just leave everything to me."

Sarah chuckled. "Why do I feel kinda naughty now?"

~~~

Even with Brian's assurance, Sarah was still nervous about doing the drop with all the women around. She hadn't had a chance to gauge the dynamic in the household yet. Carolina seemed to be the harem keeper. She handled the women and seemed to act as Victor's number two while Carlo was the houseboy and all around gopher. One thing Sarah did know was Carlo and

Carolina hooked up at every chance they got. She walked in on them having a quickie in the bathroom before the shopping trip. They invited her to join them but it looked as though they had things pretty well in hand. She begged off.

The plan was for Brian to meet her in town and give her the bugs and cameras she'd need to wire the house. With so many people and such a large house in the mix, Vince felt it was better if she had enough bugs to plant in most rooms and cameras to hide in the important places, like Victor's office and bedroom.

~~~

Sarah browsed through the handbags at the Louis Vuitton store while the other girls milled about and racked up Victor's credit card bill.

"Excuse me? I'm shopping for my girlfriend and could really use a woman's opinion."

The familiar voice with a slight Texan twang caused Sarah to smile as she turned around to see Brian impeccably dressed in a linen shirt and pants.

He had a befuddled look on his face and Sarah had to hold back a snicker.

This is one man who never shops for women.

She smiled, tossed her hair over her shoulder and gave him a flirty response. "I suppose that qualifies me to give you an opinion."

"Do you like this bag?" Brian extended a $2,100 Louis Vuitton Alma handbag exactly like the one she'd loved and lost when Hassan's boat blew up in the Mediterranean.

Sarah took a deep breath and fingered the embossed leather bag. "Yes, it is a beautiful bag. I had one like it myself once. Any woman would love it."

Brian bobbed his head in relief and sighed. "Great! Thank you so much. I really had no idea what to get for her."

A snicker sneaked out before Sarah could stop herself. She played along. "I'm sure she'll like anything you give her."

He squared his shoulders, smiled a big Texas grin and dropped his sunglasses to look her in the eyes. "Yeah, you're probably right."

Sarah watched as Brian walked over to the cashier and then busied herself looking at scarves. She couldn't help but notice that the rest of Victor's girls were watching Brian too. She laughed silently to herself.

Sorry, girls. He doesn't pay for it.

She picked a scarf she liked and walked over to the cashier after Brian left.

The clerk smiled. "Are you with Mr. Bolshoi?"

"Yes."

The cashier wrapped the silk scarf in tissue and placed it into a shopping bag already sitting on the counter. She handed Sarah the bag. "*Grazie. Buon giorno.*"

When Sarah stepped outside, she looked into the paper bag and saw the Alma handbag Brian asked her about in the store. A little thrill shot up her spine.

Yay! I get to keep the three thousand dollar handbag!

When she opened it, she saw all the electronics she would possibly need to completely wire the house and pool area.

Oh, that man has style. You can bet those Cold War spies didn't get schwag like this.

"Shall we have lunch, ladies?"

Sarah quickly closed the shopping bag at the sound of Victor's voice.

She looked up to see Victor ushering her and the three other girls into a nearby restaurant. They were shown to a large circular booth with a back so high it was practically a private room.

"Carolina and Laura, you sit on that side." Victor slid into the center seat. "On my left, I want Sarah and then Anna."

Sarah sat next to Victor as instructed. She needed to warm up to him so she had an excuse to be in his room. Without access, she wouldn't be able to plant the bugs or look for hard evidence.

Sarah sat as close to Victor as she could without being on top of him. She reached over, picked up his linen napkin from the table and whispered in his ear as she spread it over his lap. "Let me help you with that."

Victor nipped her earlobe. "It isn't the napkin I need help with." She had to separate personal feelings from work and this was work, plain and simple.

She stroked his thigh and whispered back. "I can help you with that, too."

The only thing that matters is the task at hand. Do what I have to do and don't worry about Vince. Time to charm the pants off this guy. Mojo don't fail me now.

Eighteen

Victor had his driver drop him off at a business meeting and return the girls to the villa to wait for him. Sarah saw her chance and snuck into his office but after a complete search, found nothing she could use as evidence.

This guy needs a better security consultant. I can't believe he doesn't have cameras in here.

She decided to push her luck and go to his bedroom.

There has to be some evidence here in the house.

She checked the closet first and found a ghastly green suitcase.

Why not?

She opened the case and what she saw blew her mind. She held up one of the Russian documents and scanned it for information.

I hope Chris has his earpiece in.

"Chris, are you listening?"

"Always, sweetheart."

"You won't believe this. I've got a suitcase here. Crappy quality Green alligator. Repellent choice in luggage by the way. Anyway, no surprises. It wasn't even locked."

"Spare me the fashion commentary and get to the point, Sarah."

"I've got documents in here, probably hundreds." Sarah rifled through them as she spoke. "English, Russian, French and I think this might be Dutch."

"Can you fire off some photos for me?"

"Sure. Hold on a sec." Sarah pulled her phone from her pocket and started snapping photos of the documents, sending them directly to Chris.

"Have you got them?"

"Sweet mother lode, Sarah." Chris whistled. "This is unbelievable."

Sarah was jumping up and down inside. She never thought it would be this easy.

"We've got him, don't we?"

"You bet your sweet bippy we do. Okay, put it all back and stand by for instructions."

Sarah breathed a sigh of relief as she put the suitcase back in the closet and made sure everything was as she had found it.

Last mission. Almost done.

Sarah heard the door to Victor's bedroom open. She threw the case back into the closet, spun around and flung herself onto the bed.

To her surprise, it wasn't Victor but a tangle of bodies otherwise known as Carolina and Carlo. She'd stumbled across them having sex all over the house since she arrived. It took a moment before they noticed her there.

"What are you doing in here?" Carolina seemed more curious than annoyed.

"I was just waiting for Victor." Sarah got off the bed and walked toward the door. "Please don't let me interrupt."

Carlo nudged Carolina and winked.

Carolina grinned and turned toward Sarah. "You aren't interrupting at all. In fact, we could always use a third."

Oh, hell. I knew I'd probably have to have sex with Victor but I wasn't expecting this.

"Well, I've never…"

Carolina crossed behind Sarah and ran her hands over Sarah's shoulders. "Don't worry, Sarah, we'll show you what to do."

A thrill went through Sarah.

These two are gorgeous and they want me?

She rode the self-esteem wave for a moment but, as flattered as she was, she had way too much on her mind to play along.

Carlo moved closer, facing Sarah. He trailed his fingers over her arms and down to her hands. He held her hands up to his mouth and gently kissed her palms while Carolina stroked her back.

How am I going to get out of this? Just think of it as a spa treatment. Yeah, that's it. A spa treatment.

Carolina gently kissed the nape of Sarah's neck while Carlo kissed her softly on the lips.

Oh, that's a hell of a spa.

Carlo and Carolina sandwiched Sarah as they kissed each other.

93

Carolina's hands traveled down Sarah's back and around her waist, reaching into her shorts while Carlo pulled them both closer, giving Sarah the benefit of feeling his solid erection up close.

Sarah tried not to giggle as she thought about how the boys would react to seeing this scene.

There's your Black Betty video, Brian.

With nowhere to move and pinned between two beautiful bodies, Sarah went with it. In moments, all three of them were on the bed.

Listening to this will kill Chris.

Soon Carlo turned his attentions to undressing Carolina.

When Sarah looked up, she saw Victor, standing by the door, arms crossed over his blocky, muscular chest and a smile on his face.

Sarah rolled from the bed and walked toward Victor.

His chest rose and fell as he watched her cross the floor.

She ran her hands around his waist and up his back while he snaked his hands around her back before bending to kiss her, hard.

His lips and tongue were firm and demanding.

She moved to unbuckle his belt but he stopped her.

"I have a very brief meeting I must attend. We'll finish this tonight."
He turned and ducked out the door.

Sarah looked back at Carlo and Carolina, saw her chance and ducked out as well.

They won't miss me.

~~~

Vince pushed his chair away from the table and rubbed the back of his neck. He reached for the cigarette he'd left in the ashtray and took a long drag before snuffing it out in the small glass dish.

"I gotta hand it to Victor for picking a great place to stay."

Jason paced the length of the table as he spun a 5.56mm round between his knuckles. "No kidding. Nine foot walls on three sides and open ocean on the fourth. I hate water insertions. I am not a friggin' duck."

Vince looked into his empty coffee mug willing it to refill itself. He hadn't had a good night's sleep since he left Sarah at that house three days ago. "No, we're going in the front gate. We'll be the entry team."

Angelo smiled at Jason. "I have four ducks who will take the beach and another team to go through the pedestrian door on the east side." He turned back toward Vince. "It will be easy to defend."

Vince took a deep breath and then exhaled. "Yeah, but we've got four of us and eight of you guys. We'll blow the gate while you blow the pedestrian doors and enter from the ocean side simultaneously." He pointed to each position on the map as he spoke. "One squad does a water insertion while the other two come in by truck. The explosions have to be coordinated perfectly so as to maximize the element of surprise. A violent entry coupled with speed will finish the package."

Angelo pointed to three positions in the compound. "Three armed guards on the outside are all we have to contend with and satellite surveillance will tell us where they were."

Vince lit another cigarette. "Once we're in, the GIS will secure the exterior while we enter and sweep the house."

Will stretched. "If Sarah can confirm she's gotten everyone out, the house will be a piece of cake."

Jason spoke up. "I hate to be a downer here, but I'm still not getting the warm fuzzies I like to get before an operation. Can we dead drop a weapon somewhere for Sarah?"

"Too risky." Vince took a drag off his cigarette.

Sarah.

Vince didn't want her taken hostage again like what happened in their previous mission against Hassan. Her proximity to the guy made her an easy target but sending her in was the only way they could find the dirt they needed. It always put her at risk more than the rest of them. He suppressed his anxiety with chain smoking.

Just stay safe until we get there, baby, and then take cover. This is the

last job.

"Got company." Brian stood by the door, waiting for the GIS guys to show for the final briefing before they took Victor's compound.

Seven Italians walked in and while there was a little swagger, Vince saw these guys were seasoned operators. Angelo wasn't about to pick mediocre men to pull Sarah's ass out of the fire. Vince respected him for that.

95

Vince and Angelo went over the plan with the ten other guys going in.

Four of the GIS would swim in from a small yacht just off Victor's beach.

Angelo's team would take the pedestrian door and Vince, Jason, Brian and Will would take the main gate, go in through the front door and clear the house.

~~~

"Sarah, we need to brief you." Sarah was beginning to grow used to Chris' whispering in her ear. "Are you alone?"

Sarah sat up and looked at the other girls lying by the pool. "I'm going to take a shower. I think I might do some shopping today. Anybody else up for shopping?"

The others smiled, nodded and perked up when she mentioned shopping.

Sarah walked upstairs to her room, switched on her MP3 player and turned up the speakers. "Okay, Chris. Send it."

"Hey, you."

Sarah couldn't mistake Vince's deep voice and smiled as she felt a warm wave envelope her.

Vince.

"Well, isn't this a nice surprise? What's going on?"

I never get tired of hearing your voice.

"We'll be coming by for a visit in one hour. Victor is on his way back. The GIS guys are positioning their boat now. Can you clear the house?"

Sarah closed her eyes and gave a small sigh. "Anything for you, baby."

And I do mean anything.

"Mmm…that's what I like to hear."

Sarah's body tingled whenever his voice deepened into a low growl that way. She grinned wide. "Beats a punch in the gut, right?"

Vince laughed. "You're not kiddin! See you soon, babe."

"Count on it."

Sarah slipped on a pair of shorts and stepped out into the hallway.

Carlo was walking toward her with his ever-present smile.

"Carlo?"

He stopped and touched her arm gently. "Yes, *cara*?"

Sarah turned on the charm. "I'd like some time alone with Victor. Could you take the others out shopping or something?"

I really don't want any of you in the crossfire.

He moved closer and let his hand rest on her lower back. "If it means we'll have some time alone later."

Sorry, Charlie.

Sarah had to admit this was one pretty boy toy. In another time or place, she'd be pulling him into the bedroom by his belt loops. But not today. She snaked her arms around his shoulders and let her breasts rub against his chest as she spoke in a breathy whisper. "Absolutely."

He kissed her with a promise she knew would never be fulfilled. She returned the kiss, grateful Carlo would be able to get the other girls out of the house before the fireworks began.

Nineteen

Sarah watched from her room as Carlo and the girls got into the long black Mercedes.

Ten minutes to go time. Jesus. Don't give me much time or anything.

Sarah walked down the hall and knocked lightly on the door to Victor's suite before opening it. "Victor?"

Sarah heard water draining from the bathtub. "Yes, come in." Victor walked out into the bedroom with a towel around his waist. His lips spread into a smile when he saw Sarah.

With a body like that, I'm thinking the coke issue was a bit overstated in the dossier. You don't do blow and keep that much muscle.

Sarah turned on the charm. "Hi. I was wondering if you had a little time."

"I'm all yours for…" He stopped to pick up his Rolex from the dresser and slipped it on. "Forty-five minutes and then I have to leave for an appointment with a business associate."

Sarah pouted. "Only forty-five minutes?"

He shrugged. "What is on your mind, Sarah?"

"Well…" She walked toward him and allowed herself to be attracted to the hard body in front of her. "I've been here for two days now, and I thought maybe it was time we got to know each other a little better."

He ran a hand through his wet hair, leaving it spiky and standing up in front. "I'm all for that. How do you propose we do it?" A slight lift of his eyebrow and the smile on his face told Sarah she had a green light for seduction.

Sarah ran her hands over his solid chest and rippled abs then fingered the towel at his waist. "Well, Victor, I had no idea you were so shy. My first impression of you was a man who took whatever or *whomever* he wanted.

Should I assume you aren't interested in me?" She pouted her lips and stared up at him with doe eyes.

He removed the towel. "Does this look like disinterest to you?" His massive erection was hard to miss.

If it's disinterest, it's pretty damned impressive. He's ready to rock.

Sarah took a deep breath and exhaled slowly. "No, not at all." She pressed herself against Victor and ran her hands from his ribs to his shoulders. "In fact, it is much more than I was hoping for."

Victor smiled as he bent to kiss Sarah.

How long can I keep this guy busy with foreplay?

She wrapped her arms around him and ran her fingers through the wet hair behind his ears.

His hands moved down to cup her buttocks and lift her up against his fully erect shaft.

That doesn't feel like it will be put off for long.

She squirmed enough to give him a taste of things to come as he carried her to the bed and lay on top of her.

She wrapped her legs around him and pulled him close as he removed her bathing suit top and began caressing her breasts.

Yeah, that's it. Fondle away.

She did all she could to not appear nervous about the impending siege.

Just keep him busy, Sarah.

He reached down and crept his hand into Sarah's shorts, lightly fingering the wet spot between her legs.

She moaned and pushed her hips upward. "Oh, Victor."

Sarah heard the shots fired. The *rat-tat-tat* of automatic weapons was unmistakable. Adrenaline kicked her heart rate up a notch. Victor jumped out of the bed and ran to a painting hanging on the opposite wall. He pulled it away to reveal a .38 and pointed the gun at Sarah. "You stay right there."

I hate when they point their guns at me.

Sarah tried to play dumb and frantic but she watched carefully as he pulled the suitcase out of its hiding place. "What's going on? Why are the guards shooting? What are you doing?"

"You know damned well why they're shooting. Who do you work for?"

Time for a tap dance.

Sarah's face dropped as part of the act. She'd have to do whatever she could to distract him until the entry team came in and took him down.

"I told you I'm a student. The only work I do is on this body." She stood up from the bed and put her bathing suit top back on. "Look, I figured you did some questionable business, but I never thought it was any of *my* business.

And I sure as hell didn't think it would be coming home with you. I was invited here for a good time, but it looks to me like the good time ended about thirty seconds ago. Now please tell me how I can get the hell out of this place!"

"Don't worry, you'll be coming with me." He grabbed for her arm but she dodged him.

Her blood started pumping double-time. Somebody was running up the stairs and they sounded heavy. "I don't think so!" She positioned herself behind a chair to block his reach and had a clear view of the window that perfectly reflected the doorway. "Those bullets aren't looking for me, sweetie!"

If I can just keep his eyes on me instead of the doorway, they can drop him when they come in.

He reached for her again but she pushed the chair into his shins. "*Aargh!*"

Sarah's eyes became two angry slits and she assumed a fighting stance. "Don't touch me!"

She saw the reflection of a shadow passing the doorway.

Yes, they're here!

Victor must have seen it too and turned toward the doorway with his handgun leveled.

Sarah pushed the chair at him one more time. This time it made his knees buckle.

Something stung Sarah's shoulder and she stumbled slightly. As she spun around to look at Victor, she saw his eyes open so wide there was white all the way around. Then a dot appeared at the top of his nose, right between his eyes, and a huge red shadow appeared on the wall behind him. He fell like a wet rag.

Nice shot.

Sarah turned to see who fired. Vince and Brian were just inside the doorway with smoking guns. Will and Jason were behind them, guns drawn on the dead heap that used to be Victor.

Vince's voice was clear as he stood. "Jesus, Sarah!"

His stare and a burning sensation in Sarah's shoulder made her look down. The left side of her body was covered in blood from the shoulder down. Everything seemed to happen in slow motion after that. She touched the hole from where the blood was flowing. She felt the warm, silky, crimson fluid between her fingers.

She looked into Vince's brown eyes. "Oh, shit." Her knees fell out from under her.

Vince lunged to catch Sarah and gently lowered her to the floor, resting her head on his thigh. "Will!"

So, this is what a gunshot wound feels like? I'll be damned.

All Sarah could see were Vince's soft, kind eyes looking down at her.

"Stay with me, Sarah."

Of course.

She half smiled. "All you had to do was ask." She wondered how bad the exit wound was and the scars she'd have.

Oh, vanity, thy name is woman.

"You're gonna fix me up nice, right Will? No scars."

Will was ripping bandages open with his teeth. "Real nice, baby. Just relax and keep talking."

Everything in her peripheral vision started to fade out.

Here it comes. Loss of consciousness.

She looked into Vince's eyes. "Don't worry. You can't get rid of me." The tunnel of her sight grew smaller and smaller. All she saw was Vince.

His eyes were so intense. The look on his face was all but relaxed. Then everything faded to black.

~~~

Vince went on autopilot as he pressed the heel of his hand against Sarah's wound. "Chris, we need the chopper now. Sarah's been shot."

Will lifted her to bandage the exit wound. "Tell the hospital we have a close range gunshot wound, but it was a .38 so it's a big one. She's lost a lot of blood. Pulse is weak. She's unconscious." Will felt her forehead—cold and clammy. "And she's going into shock."

101

Will finished bandaging and looked at Vince. "Let's get her out of here."

Vince picked Sarah up and carried her as quickly as his legs would take him, through the house and down the stairs. When he got outside, Jason was already in the side yard and popped a smoke canister to signal the chopper.

Vince looked down at Sarah's limp body. His heart ached and his stomach rolled. "Come on, Sarah. Can you hear me? You're gonna be fine."

The smell of the smoke mixed with the sea air brought back memories he knew he shouldn't focus on.

This isn't the same. Sarah is fine. We'll get her to the hospital and she'll be fine.

"You're gonna be fine. Just hang on."

Vince pulled Sarah's face close to his chest as the force from the chopper threw sand and gravel at them. He ran toward the chopper and put Sarah on the floor inside. He knelt at her head, keeping his finger on her pulse the whole time.

Jason's voice came from the door. "We got one more!"

Oh, no.

The last thing Vince wanted was more casualties today. He looked out the side door to see Brian and Will carrying Angelo. "Where's he hit?"

Oh, hell. The Italians aren't going to be happy about this.

Angelo's face was pale but he was conscious. "Sarah?"

Vince looked at Angelo, so pale, with sweat beading down his face and neck. He wasn't going to make it. Vince spoke loudly so Angelo could hear him over the police radios and helicopter rotors. "Shoulder. Will patched her up. She'll be fine."

But you won't.

Will continued to work over Angelo, trying to bandage the abdominal wound. "Chris, we've got another casualty. Multiple gunshots to the abdomen. It's Angelo. He's lost a lot of blood."

Vince never liked the idea of competing with Angelo. He was a good guy and damned good at his job. Vince liked him and it was a real kick in the nuts to see him take that last bullet right before he was about to retire.

He deserved better than this.

Angelo's breathing was shallow and his eyes were growing cloudy. "Keep her safe. Make her happy, Vincenzo." He grabbed Vince's hand and squeezed it. "Promise me."

"*Ti prometto.*"

Angelo squeezed Vince's hand one more time and nodded. Vince felt Angelo let go and watched as he closed his eyes and took his last breath.

Will tried to perform CPR but the blood never made it to Angelo's brain. His wounds were too extensive. Will stopped pumping Angelo's chest and his shoulders sank as he knelt over the dead man. He rubbed his face with bloody hands. "She's okay, right?"

Vince grabbed his shoulder and looked him in the eye. "Sarah is fine. You patched her up. She's weak but she's going to be fine. Angelo was too far gone. There was nothing you could do."

Will sat back against the closed door of the chopper. "I know. I know. I just never get used to it."

Vince said a silent prayer for Sarah. "If you did, you wouldn't be human."

Twenty

The firm grip of Will's hand on his shoulder woke Vince. "Is she awake?"

"No."

"Boss, you need some sleep. Why don't you go back to the house and I'll sit with her. Jason and Brian will be here in a few hours. We'll take care of her."

"No, Will. This is my fault. I did this to her. I have to stay."

"Vince, you're holding on too tight. This is an occupational hazard. You'll see it clearly after you get some rest."

"No." He touched her pale cheek. "I have to stay with her."

"Alright. I'll go get us some coffee." Will turned to go but stopped as the doctor entered the room.

Vince turned around to look at the doctor but kept one hand on Sarah's just in case she woke up. His shoulders slumped with the weight of worry. Sarah had been asleep too long. "She's still not awake. Is that normal?"

"She's suffered a severe trauma. It is natural for her body to conserve energy."

Will rubbed his chin. "What about the scars? She's not gonna be happy about scars when she wakes up."

She's definitely not vain, but he's absolutely right about that. She won't like scars.

"It was a very clean wound. The scarring will be minimal."

"Okay, that's good." Will nodded. "When can we expect her to regain consciousness?"

"We gave her a strong sedative. It will be a few more hours."

"Thank you, doctor." Will looked over his shoulder at Vince. "I'll go see about that coffee."

~~~

Sarah woke from a deep sleep. Somebody was snoring. Several somebodies were snoring. Chris lay cramped on a small sofa in the corner, Jason sprawled in a chair with his feet on Brian's chair, and from his slouch in a second chair, Brian had his feet braced on the foot of the bed.

What am I doing in bed?

Somebody was holding her hand. She felt a dull pain as she turned her head.

Vince sat in a chair by her bed, his head rested on his well muscled arm.

He held her hand with both of his.

She could barely whisper. "Vince?"

Vince jumped as though he had been slapped in the face. A hoarse whisper escaped his lips. "Hey, sweetheart." He smiled but he was haggard.

The beard growth gave away the fact he clearly hadn't shaved in days.

Brian woke next. He nudged Chris and Jason before moving to the foot of Sarah's bed. "Hey, darlin. Nice of you to join us."

Sarah panicked when she realized somebody was missing. "Where's Will? Is he alright? Oh, my God, did he get shot, too?"

Will strolled into the room looking fresh as a daisy and carrying a tray of coffee cups.

Sarah sighed with relief.

Will smiled a broad, clean-shaven smile. "Hey, look who finally decided to wake up!"

Sarah squeezed Vince's hand. "Everybody okay?"

"Yeah, yeah, we're okay. How do you feel?"

"I'm sore. What happened?"

Vince kissed Sarah's hand. "You were shot."

Sarah caressed his cheek. "Vince, you look like hell."

Will slapped Vince on the back. "Yeah, sitting in these chairs for a couple days will do that to a man." Will looked directly at Vince. "She's awake now and we're here. Why don't you go clean up and get some rest, man?"

"No. I need to talk to Sarah. You guys go get some breakfast or something."

"Vince, you don't have to do this now."

"Yeah, we need to."

"Okay boys, let's bounce." Brian, Chris and Jason followed Will quickly out of the room.

"Vince, what's going on?"

"Sarah, you weren't the only one hit when we raided the compound."

"But the guys look fine. You?"

"No, the boys and I made it without a scratch but Angelo wasn't so lucky."

"Where is he? Is he here?"

"No, Sarah. I'm sorry. He didn't make it."

Oh, no. Oh, God, no!

Twenty-One

Sarah watched Chris walk out onto the patio with a puzzled look on his face and a large envelope in his hand.

"What's wrong, Chris?"

He held up the envelope. "This just came for you by messenger. It's from Angelo's lawyers."

Sarah's stomach turned. She felt terrible staying in Angelo's home while she recuperated, but the GIS insisted the team stay there for security reasons. "I can't imagine what it is. Would you read it, please?"

Chris sat in the chair near Sarah and opened the envelope. He started reading to himself. After a long minute, he looked up at Sarah with sadness in his eyes. "It is his will. He left it all to you."

"Chris, what are you talking about?"

"The estate, the groves, the house, the cars. All of it along with significant investments that have historically brought in, well…" Chris pointed to a figure on the page. "This much, annually."

"Oh, dear God!" Sarah slumped back in her chair and threw her hand onto her upturned forehead. Tears began rolling down her cheeks almost instantly.

"Whoa, whoa, whoa!" Vince was kneeling in front of her in a flash.

Sarah sobbed forward into Vince's arms. "He thought…"

Will, Brian, Jason and Chris all walked quietly into the house.

Vince wrapped his arms protectively around her and pushed the tear dampened hair from her face. Vince's voice was low and soft. "Don't go there, Sarah. He thought you'd be happy here. He wanted you to be happy."

She sobbed into Vince's shoulder. "He thought I was going to marry him."

"Shh…no, Sarah. He knew. He wanted you to be safe and happy. That was all he wanted."

Sarah picked her head up and tried to catch her breath. "But?"

"He told me."

Sarah took a short breath and looked into Vince's eyes. "What?"

Vince blinked and looked into the quiet blue sky above them for a moment. His gaze met Sarah's. "The man grabbed my hand like a vise and made me promise to keep you safe and happy. All that time I hated him for being so good and cool and having the balls to ask you to marry him. Turns out, he really was a good guy and he did care about you. He just wanted you to be happy, and he thought you might be happy here."

Sarah took a deep breath and wiped the tears rolling from her eyes. "What an unselfish and wonderful thing to do."

Vince stroked her hair as she let herself grieve for Angelo.

When exhaustion set in and the tears stopped, she looked up at Vince. "Where did the guys go?"

"Like I told you from the start, they get nervous around weepy women. They went inside."

Sarah wiped her eyes with her good hand while the other rested in a sling to keep her from moving her wounded shoulder. "Well, let's go in there and talk about this."

Vince put his arm around her waist. "Sarah, you've been through a lot. You need time to think clearly. The guys know you're overwhelmed. They've seen us together. They know what's coming."

Sarah straightened and took a deep breath. "Let's go."

Vince nodded and followed.

Will was the first to speak. "You okay, kid?"

Sarah sat in the large leather chair. "Yeah, sit down guys. Let's talk.'

Vince stood beside her chair. "Take your time, Sarah. There's no need to talk to anyone about anything. This place is yours. End of story."

"Okay, boys. What do I do with this?"

"At the risk of sounding insensitive," Will lit a cigar, "you got it all now, pork chop. You've got the body, money, a great place in Vegas, and now an estate in Italy. This would be a good time to cash in your chips."

Sarah looked at Brian.

"You've got your back up plan and your retirement hooked up now. This is a good thing."

Jason fidgeted with his Zippo. "Nobody would hold it against you if you quit the business now. Frankly, the thought of seeing you shot again makes me pretty nervous."

Chris ran his fingers through his hair, his nervous tell. "Sarah, why don't you take some convalescent leave, talk to a lawyer and then give this some thought. I'll be honest, I'd be hard pressed to leave a life like this."

Sarah stood. She had to move to keep pace with her thoughts.

What does this mean? What happened?

She lit a cigarette with a shaky hand, smoking and pacing while the guys watched silently.

Her mind raced to grasp it all. She spoke to slow her brain. "A man I barely knew gave me a mansion on an estate that brings in a bigger annual income than I could imagine earning in a lifetime. He worked thirty years to keep people safe and happy and when it was his time to just relax and enjoy life he took a bullet? It doesn't make any sense." She turned and looked into Vince's soft brown eyes. "Is this how it ends for all of us? We fight so hard for other people to have a happy ending and instead of a gold watch, we get a bullet?"

Vince shook his head. "Sarah. You're upset. It's a lot to take in all at once."

"A lot to take in? That's an understatement!" She turned and paced some more. "Tapestries. Artwork. Antiques. I have a fucking ballroom for fuck's sake!" Sarah's face went white as a sheet. She started to sway.

Vince jumped up and caught her before she fell.

"Okay, sweetheart. Let's sit down." He placed her in one of the large leather chairs and knelt in front of her. "You aren't doing this today. You're still recovering. You haven't eaten in days. You need to rest. That's an order."

Her eyes were glazed over. The lack of sleep, the meds and the stress were too much right now.

"Yes, I think I should go to bed. I'm sorry I flipped. It's been a big day." She moved to stand but her knees just couldn't hold out.

Vince caught her and she collapsed against him. He carried her up the stairs to the master bedroom, her bedroom, and his heart ached for the woman quietly weeping in his arms.

"He was a good man, Vince. I didn't love him, but he was one of the good guys."

"Yes, he was. He was definitely one of the good guys."

"I'm so tired."

Vince laid her on the bed and covered her with a blanket. "Get some sleep." He kissed her on the forehead.

She grabbed his hand. "Vince, don't leave me."

He sat on the edge of the bed, brushed the hair from her face as her breathing slowed and he knew she drifted off. "Never."

Twenty-Two

Pain shot through her shoulder. *"Aargh!"* Sarah couldn't help but shout out with the pain. She sat up and looked at the bedside clock.

Hard, heavy footsteps ran down the hallway at the same pace as the beat of her heavily thumping heart.

Vince stormed into the room and scanned it, Sig in hand. "What happened? Are you alright?"

"Oh, my God, Vince!" Sarah flopped back down on the pillow with a wince. "I'm okay. I overslept and haven't taken anything for the pain in about fourteen hours. I rolled over onto my side in my sleep and felt it. That's all." She chuckled. "That response was in record time, Marine. You're pretty fast for an old guy."

Vince tucked the sidearm into his belt and sat beside Sarah. "You wanna see fast? Just wait until that shoulder heals. I'll show you what an old guy can do."

"Promises. Prom…"

Vince stopped her with a kiss. "That is a promise I will most definitely keep." He stood and walked to the dresser. "You need some help getting dressed? The guys are leaving today."

Sarah kicked the sheet off and stepped out of the bed. "I don't understand why they have to leave so soon."

Vince helped her slip a shirt on over her bandaged shoulder. "We milked the Italian debrief period as long as we could. Young would only authorize one of us to stay behind until you're cleared by the doctor and ready to fly."

"Couldn't you play the whole 'teams stay together' card? Surely you could have thrown that team effort shit at him."

"I tried, babe." Vince shrugged. "A six-two, two-twenty guy can't pull that off as well as a five-ten, buck fifty knockout like you. Besides, I was on the phone, and batting my eyelashes doesn't carry the same weight as it does in person."

Sarah giggled at the thought of Vince batting his eyelashes for anyone.

She kissed him on the cheek. "Point taken. Looks like I'm stuck with you then, huh?"

"At least thirty or forty years." Vince followed her as she walked downstairs.

"It's about time, darlin'." Brian's bright smile greeted Sarah as she walked down the stairs. "We thought we were going to have to leave without saying goodbye."

"Don't you ever do that, Brian." Sarah wrapped her good arm around him in a tight hug and kissed him on the cheek.

When Brian stepped aside, Jason was there with open arms and his devilish grin. "It's just not going to be the same without you to kick around every day. Get better and come back soon, okay?"

Sarah hugged him back. "No bar fights without me, okay?"

"Okay, but you really do need to hurry. You know how I like my brawls."

Chris scowled when Sarah moved to hug him goodbye.

"Why the sad face?"

"I still need a golf partner. It's going to take forever to break in a new one. Just how long are you going to milk this handicap?"

Sarah chuckled. "There's just no budging your priorities, is there?"

Chris hugged her, careful not to squeeze her bad shoulder. "It's all I've got."

Will shook Vince's hand. "Take your time, man. There's no need to rush back. See that our girl comes back safely."

"No worries there." Vince pulled Will in for a one-armed hug.

A car horn sounded outside.

Sarah gave Will a kiss on the cheek. "I don't do long goodbyes so get the hell out of here. I'll see you bums when the doc clears me in a few days."

Brian picked up his bags. "You talk a good game, darlin', but you know you're going to cry yourself to sleep when we leave."

Sarah opened the door. "There will be tears and lots of blubbering. Be safe, guys."

Chris and Jason responded in unison on their way out. "Yes, dear."

"You don't look so good." Vince watched Sarah as she closed the door.

"I'll be alright. Did the guys leave any coffee?"

"I think Isabella made another pot for you. Why don't you go sit on the patio? I'll get the coffee. How about some breakfast and something for the pain too?"

Sarah turned to Vince and kissed him lightly on the lips. "No. Just the coffee now. I'll be fine. Thank you."

If I didn't have this hole in my shoulder, I'd be in heaven right now.

She walked through the quiet house that had been so busy when the guys were still there. It still hadn't sunk in that this beautiful mansion was all hers. She walked out to the patio and sat on one of the chaise lounges by the pool.

Vince set a cup of coffee and a pill on the table next to her. "Just in case you need it."

She grabbed his hand. "Really. I'm fine. I don't even think I need this sling anymore." She slipped her arm out and pulled it over her head. A twinge of pain shot through her shoulder but she tried not to let it show.

Vince sat next to her on the other chaise and sighed. "Sarah, you've been shot. You don't have to suck it up. I'm not going to think less of you if you take something for the pain. Just take the meds, please?"

She held his hand and leaned back. "I don't want this memory to be clouded in a pharmaceutical haze. I want to remember every bit of this."

"Take the pill, woman. I promise we have plenty of time to make clear memories, and we will."

She looked into his eyes and the pain went away. Somehow, all of this seemed so right. She took the pill with a swig of coffee and closed her eyes as she faced the warm midday sun.

~~~

"You're gonna burn out here."

"Mmm…"

A hand touched her cheek and she leaned into it.

"Sarah?"

"Mmm…"

Sarah felt his breath on her cheek

This dream seems so real.

His lips touched hers and she realized it wasn't the dream. The sound of the ocean was real. The palm trees whispering in the breeze were real.

The man next to her was real. It wasn't a dream any more. The sun shone down and warmed her body. The air was fresh and warm as she breathed deeply. All was right in her world now. He was there. She heard him breathing ever so quietly. She turned to him and opened her eyes.

Thank God, I'm not dreaming this time.

Vince was there, smiling at her. "You've been asleep for hours. Was it a good dream?"

"Very good. It isn't a dream anymore." Sarah touched his face and pulled him closer.

His lips met hers gently at first. Tentative. Tender. He reached around her and softly pulled her closer to him. His lips were more demanding now.

She stroked his neck, his shoulders, his arm. Her fingers mapped every inch they touched. She'd waited too long for this.

Too soon, he pulled away and stood up.

"Vince?"

He picked her up in his arms. His eyes softened and a look of pain came over his face.

"What is it?"

He barely spoke in a whisper. "I can't get that image of you, bloody and unconscious, out of my head. I thought I'd lost you."

"Never, Vince. Never." Sarah wiped a grateful tear from her eye.

His smile was indulgent but said he knew otherwise.

"Now you listen to me. Not a bullet, not a million miles. You'll never lose me." Vince carried her inside, set her gently on her bed and began undressing her.

She wanted him. It was always him. It always would be. She didn't need a man to complete her, but she needed this man in her life to realize it.

Now she could give herself to this man without losing her soul For the first time in her life, she could give herself completely without losing herself in the process.

Twenty-Three

Vince watched Sarah as she opened her eyes.

She snuggled closer to him with a sleepy smile. "Good morning."

"Yes, it is. Uh…do you remember last night?"

She kissed his chest. "How could I forget? Do you have regrets?"

"Are you kidding? This is the first time in years I woke up with a woman and didn't want to gnaw my arm off to escape."

Sarah winced. "Compliment?"

Vince rolled his eyes. "Very much so. How about I get us some coffee and we spend the morning in bed?"

"Oh, God yes!"

Vince slipped on his jeans and walked downstairs to the kitchen. He pulled a carafe from the cupboard and started filling it with the coffee Isabella had made.

The low buzz of his cell phone pulled his focus from the coffee. He pulled the phone from his pocket and flipped it open with a smile. "Morning, Chris."

Chris was tentative. "Vince, I got some bad news and you're not gonna like it."

Vince's smile melted away and he rolled his shoulders back, preparing himself for yet another crisis. "Isn't that the meaning of bad news? Get to it, Chris."

"The team assigned to take out Nikolai didn't."

"What do you mean they didn't? It isn't a one-shot deal. You follow him into hell if you have to. You chase the son of a bitch down until you kill him."

"Uh, Vince." Chris paused.

Vince knew Chris was probably scratching his head, doing that nervous fidget he did when he had bad news. "I'm tired of dancing with you, Chris. Sarah is waiting for her coffee, and she can be downright bitchy if she doesn't get it. Just say what you have to say."

"The team is gone. All, but one, were gunned down in their safe house."

What the fuck?

"Are you shitting me? The whole team?" Vince knew Nikolai's connections were heavy but for him to escape when Victor hadn't was a very bad sign.

We had the organization mapped all wrong.

If Nikolai knew about the bust on Victor, as well as the team following him, then he had to be higher up on the food chain than Victor. Much higher.

"Jesus, Chris. You know what that means?"

"Yeah, they gave us a bad organizational chart among other things."

"We've got a hot one who knows who we are and what we do. We've been made."

Chris sighed. "I know. What do you want us to do now?"

"You and Brian get to the Camp. Make sure you aren't followed. Put Will and Jason on a private flight to escort Sarah. Do it now." Vince hung up on Chris and hit a speed dial key.

A woman's voice answered. "Swift Imports. How may I help you?"

"It's Hennessee, priority."

Young's gravelly voice answered on the first ring. "Hey, Vince. Nice work on the Russian. We got some great stuff here."

Vince paced across the kitchen as he talked. "Save the bullshit, Young. What happened with Nikolai?"

"The team was compromised. Only one made it out alive and he was supposed to be the shooter."

"Why didn't he take Nikolai?"

"He lost Nikolai right before his team went down."

Vince ran his hand over his head. "They could, hell, they will target *my* team next."

"Yeah. I'm afraid that is a possibility. How do you want to handle it?"

"Have temporary quarters made up for the team at the Camp. Chris and Brian are on their way. Sarah is still recuperating in Italy so Jason and Will are coming to get her. I'll be in touch." Vince hung up and hit another speed dial key to call Will.

Will answered the phone before the first ring had finished. "Adams."

"Did Chris brief you?"

"Yeah. The boys and I are packing now. Chris is meeting us here."

Vince gave a small sigh of relief. He heard a handgun being cleared and loaded in the background.

They'll be fine.

"What about you and Sarah?"

"She'll be okay until you and Jason get here. I'll have a couple GIS guys bunk in until you arrive. Tell Jason to pack heavy. Nikolai knows who she is, and she'll be a prime target. I'll make sure the GIS knows you're coming in loaded so they can clear it with customs."

"What about you?"

Vince rubbed his chin. "I gotta go solo on this. He's expecting a team."

"I don't like it, brother. I'll go with you."

"No. You need to take care of the team. You're in charge now. Once we nail Nikolai, Sarah and I are out."

Will sighed. "Alright, but I need daily status checks."

"No problem." A phone call every day to make sure he was safe was exactly what he would have required. Vince hated the position they were in, but he was relieved to know Sarah and the boys were in good hands with Will taking the lead.

"Watch your six, leatherneck."

"Always." Vince hung up with Will and immediately called Angelo's commander to brief him of the situation. He was given the names and descriptions of two GIS officers who would arrive shortly to guard Sarah while she waited for Will and Jason to arrive. He passed on the details to Isabella in case they came in while he was talking to Sarah.

Now to tell Sarah. What the hell do I tell Sarah?

Vince didn't want to lie, but he knew if he told her the truth she would want to come along and wouldn't take no for an answer.

I have to lie.

Vince finished pouring the coffee as Sarah walked into the kitchen. He gave her a kiss on the cheek. "Hey, I was just on my way up. Are you okay?"

Sarah smiled and walked toward the table. "Yeah, I'm fantastic. You took a while so I thought I'd better hunt you down."

Vince pulled a chair from the table for her. "Good instincts. Have a seat. I need to talk to you."

~~~

Sarah blinked hard and cleared her throat. She knew the goodbye was coming. A lead ball formed in her stomach. "So when do you have to leave?"

Vince sighed and held her free hand across the table. "I've got a deal to put together in the U.A.E. this week. I'm flying out this afternoon."

A sharp pain stabbed at her chest, and Sarah drew a quick breath. The bullet wound didn't hurt nearly as much as his leaving.

Vince jumped out of his chair and appeared by her side in a flash. "Sarah, are you alright?"

"Yeah, I'm fine. Just a little tender." She stood so she could be closer to him, if for only a few more minutes.

Vince wrapped his arms around her and cleared his throat. "Listen, since I have to go, I'm having Will and Jason come get you. I don't want you staying here by yourself."

"Why? The estate is secure. Angelo had a state of the art security system and there's a guard monitoring it. I have a staff if I want company. I don't need Will and Jason here to amuse me."

"I just think it would be best. Please trust me on this?"

Sarah looked over Vince's shoulder to see two Italian police standing in the next room. "Vince, who are those guys in the sitting room?"

"They're with the GIS. Angelo had some things in his office. They're just gonna hang around until Will and Jason get here."

My bullshit meter is going off the charts. Protection. They're here for protection.

"Who are they here to protect me from?"

Vince stepped back, pulled a box of cigarettes from his cargo pocket and dropped his head. "Jesus, woman." He tapped a cigarette from the box and lit it. His eyes met hers and she could see he was trying to keep the truth from her. "Why can't you just go with the story?" His shoulders dropped in defeat.

"Because your storytelling sucks. We agreed we're leaving this job together and now you tell me you're working on some deal in the U.A.E.? Either this is a really over the top way of dumping me now that you've had me, or some shit has hit the fan and you're on the clean-up crew. No bullshit now." Sarah braced for bad news and waited for Vince to tell her what was really going on.

He took a deep breath and exhaled before beginning. "We got a bad organizational chart from intel. It turns out Nikolai was higher up than Victor and we got made. The team in Russia that was supposed to take him down got hit and there was only one survivor. He didn't get Nikolai." He ran a hand over his head. "You and the guys are going to bunk at the Camp for a few days until we can get a bead on Nikolai and clean this up."

Sarah didn't like what "you guys" meant. It implied Vince's absence. "And where will you be?"

Vince took a long drag from the Marlboro and exhaled loudly. He looked into her eyes and touched her cheek. "I'll be the one getting the bead."

Twenty-Four

At the sound of the car horn, Sarah followed Vince outside. The taxi was waiting. An emptiness inside threatened to eat her.

One more goodbye. When will they stop?

Vince stopped just outside the front door and turned to face her. He took her hand in his. "Goodbyes are so awkward."

"Then don't say goodbye." Sarah's stomach churned and dread washed over her. "Just don't say it."

Something tells me I'm not going to see him again.

Vince dropped his bag and reached around Sarah's waist pulling her close. "I'll finish this soon and then it'll be sweet liberty with breakfast in bed and lunch by the pool every day."

She ran her right hand up his chest and around his neck. "And the hammock. Don't forget the hammock."

Vince pulled her closer. "Yeah, you're gonna look good in that hammock."

Sarah nuzzled his neck. "You paint a nice picture, leatherneck. Just watch your six and come back alive."

"Always." Vince touched her lips gently with his then whispered in her ear, "I love you."

Before his words registered in her mind, Vince grabbed his bag, ducked into the taxi and told the driver to go.

Sarah closed her eyes and said a little prayer for his safety before turning to walk back into the house. "I love you too."

~~~

Vince stepped out of the taxi and shouldered his bag. He looked around to see what other cars were arriving behind him, then handed the driver a handful of bills for the ride and walked into the airport terminal. He scanned the crowd for anyone who looked suspicious.

Too many people. Too many to tell.

He checked the monitors for the next flight to Moscow.

That'll be the place to start if he doesn't find me first.

Vince made his way to the Czech Airlines desk and purchased a one-way ticket. The attendant seemed distracted.

Not a good sign.

The hairs on the back of Vince's neck stood on end. He took a quick look around before accepting the boarding pass she handed him and started making his way to the departure area. Vince just passed through security when he felt something hard in the small of his back.

Shit.

"Don't cause a scene. See that door to your left?"

"Yeah."

"Walk through it."

Vince walked through the service door and looked for anything he could use as a weapon.

Everything went black.

~~~

Isabella laid out a beautiful dinner on the patio in honor of Will and Jason's arrival. Sarah had to admit she loved having Isabella there to manage the house. Because she'd worked so long for Angelo and was cleared by the GIS, Sarah thought it was only right to keep her on.

The patio was quiet and none of them spoke much. Sarah guessed they were probably just as concerned about Vince as she was. They had just begun to eat their dinner when Isabella walked out onto the patio. "Signor Adams, there is a phone call for you in the study."

"Thank you, Isabella." Will shot Sarah a curious glance as he left the table.

Something pulled at Sarah's gut. She gave Jason the same curious glance. "Who would call him here?"

Jason shook his head. "This can't be good." He pulled a Beretta out from under his pant leg and set it on the table between his plate and Sarah's.

There was something she and Jason both found reassuring about cold steel with the safety off.

After what seemed like hours, Will returned and collapsed in his chair. He tossed the rest of his Scotch down in one gulp, took a deep breath and delivered a body blow. "That was an agency friend in Rome. I've got good news and bad news." He pushed his fingers through his hair and held his head for a moment while staring at nothing in particular.

Will always has it together. Whatever the bad news is, it must be really bad.

Sarah set her wine glass down with a shaky hand. She and Jason both spoke at the same time. "Bad news."

"Now we know why Vince hasn't called. He's been kidnapped."

Sarah's eyes opened wide. "He what?"

Nobody kidnaps a Marine!

"Yeah, a couple guys took him at gunpoint from the airport. A core collector for the agency in Saudi got wind that a couple guys brought him into the country on a private airstrip. We know the agency will disavow any connection with him if a ransom is demanded. So far, none has."

Sarah came unglued. "Well we can't just let him disappear like that! What are we going to do about this? What can we do? Will, can this *friend* of yours help us?"

Jason put a calming hand on Sarah's shoulder. "Hold on. Let's get the whole story, Sarah."

Will continued. "You'll never guess who the strip belongs to."

Jason sighed. "Nikolai."

"Yeah. That's all the information my guy passed on. Young was informed of this about two hours ago and instructed to share none of it with us."

"So Young won't be any help." Jason leaned forward on his elbows.

"Right."

"So what's the good news, Will?" Sarah would take anything at this point.

"The good news is there is a guy at the embassy in Saudi who can tell us where Vince is."

Sarah felt a wave of relief. "Ok, so we know where he is. What do we do now?" She leaned forward and watched Will closely so she wouldn't miss a word.

"Sarah, you're already on convalescent leave. Jason and I are technically on vacation while we're staying with you here." Will rolled up the sleeves of his Oxford. "I've already called Chris and he and Brian are both taking some vacation time effective immediately. As far as Young knows, we're all enjoying some down time in Italy while we're reviewing resumes of possible replacements."

Jason jumped in, "…while we're actually planning to kidnap Vince back."

"So now we go to Saudi Arabia. You call the jet. I'll call my driver." Sarah reached for her phone but Will stopped her with a gentle hand on hers.

"No. Security is tight there and that works to Nikolai's benefit. It'll be easier for us to fly into Dubai. The real estate market there has taken a major dump so we can go in looking like investors, get the royal treatment and nobody's going to question why we're there. Chris already made reservations at the Burj al Arab, and he and Brian will meet us there. We leave in the morning."

Jason raised a pensive finger. "That's all well and good, and props on putting this all together while Sarah and I had our salads, but we're gonna need gear. We're gonna need weapons. How are we going to get all that shit into Dubai?"

"We aren't." Will's eyes sparkled. "It's already there."

"How?"

"Vince's island."

Sarah gasped. "He really does have an island?" She blinked slowly as she tried to wrap her brain around the fact that her boyfriend owned an island.

"We've used it a few times for stopovers while we were doing arms deals." Will nodded. "It's got everything we'll need."

"Excellent." Jason attacked his steak as though his life depended on it. He always had a hankering for steak right before a mission so why should this be any different?

Eat up, Jase. Vince is going to need all the help he can get and you are definitely an army of one when you're well fed.

Twenty-Five

Sarah woke to yet another sunny day it Italy. The sleepless night did nothing to ease the ravages of stress but Will needed the few hours to make phone calls, transfer money and prepare for a mission that was completely off the books.

This is all wrong. Here I am living in the lap of luxury with everything I have ever wanted, and the two men who freely gave of themselves to me are worse off than before they met me. Angelo is dead and Vince is missing.

Sarah slipped on a smart black dress and the pearls Vince gave her. She could honor them both.

She closed the suitcase she'd packed the night before and stowed the last of her toiletries in the square Louis Vuitton case. She slung her carry-on bag over her shoulder, took a piece of luggage in each hand and walked slowly down the stairs. She made a point to take in all the elegance and beauty that represented her freedom from material want. Will and Jason's bags were already stacked neatly on the marble floor of the entryway. The antique table looked less festive now, topped with the eighteen-inch marble vase that stood cold and empty, without flowers.

She arranged her bags by Will and Jason's and walked into the kitchen.

She braced herself with her good hand on the marble countertop and sighed as she admired the view from the window.

Just stay alive, Vince.

She poured a cup of coffee, steeled herself with a deep breath and joined the guys on the patio.

They both stood and Jason pulled a chair from the table for her.

Ah, chivalry is not dead.

"Morning, Sarah." Jason smiled.

"Good morning, Jase. Morning, Will."

"Good morning. How's the shoulder?"

Sarah sat and took a sip of her coffee. "Not bad. I can carry a little weight without any problem. My physical therapist says I can get back to working out now."

Will nodded. "That's good." They finished their coffee in silence.

Just as Sarah put her empty cup down on the table, Isabella came out to announce their car was waiting.

"*Grazie*, Isabella."

"Have a good trip, Miss Stevens."

Busting my boyfriend out of a compound in Saudi Arabia where he's being held by one of the world's biggest arms dealers. Not exactly, the kind of trip a girl wants to make.

Sarah nodded and took a deep breath. "Thank you,

Isabella. I'll call you when I'm on my way back." She stood and walked through her new home for the last time in what may be a long while.

Who knows how long I'll be gone?

The guys walked outside with the luggage as Sarah took one last look at her beautiful home.

That taste of liberty was wonderful. We made some sweet memories, Vince. Thank you, Angelo.

She wiped a lone tear from her cheek and sighed.

As though a promise to the man she loved and the other who had given her so much, a whisper escaped her lips. "Somebody's gonna die."

Enjoy A Sneak Peek Of Freedom's Promise, Book 3 in the Task Force 125 Series

One

Vince Hennessee woke with a start and gasped to find himself sitting in a heavy wooden chair, unable to move. He fought the urge to panic and took a deep breath to calm himself. He tried to kick his feet but they wouldn't budge. Rolling his shoulders, he tugged at the bindings on his wrists.

Duct tape?

He squinted through the dark and made out a few furnishings with the small bit of available natural light coming from the windows. Blinking hard, he wondered what they'd drugged him with. Fighting to focus and remember what happened, he could not will the mental fog away.

Where am I, and how the hell did I get here?

Vince squeezed his eyes shut and opened them again, trying to remember what had happened. Images of being abducted at the airport in Italy flitted through his mind. He'd been on his way to Moscow to meet with Mark Davidson to track down Nikolai.

Somebody hit me, drugged me, and brought me here. But where is here?

Vince knew he had to stay calm, assess the situation, and not do anything foolish. His years as a Recon Marine, seeing more than his share of action in world hot spots, had taught him to remain calm above all else.

His focus was clearer now that the effects of the drug were wearing off and more light shone through the windows.

Sunrise somewhere.

He scanned the room to see mother-of-pearl and gold inlaid on the sideboard, a white marble floor, dark Persian rugs, and Byzantine style windows.

The hairs on the back of his neck bristled as somewhere outside and far off a Muezzin began the Muslim call to prayer. He'd always found the chanting at prayer times moving, but today it was just eerie.

I'm in the Middle East again, but where?

Vince remembered the last time he'd been held hostage in the Middle East. He quickly locked the memory in the back of his mind and forced himself to focus on the present.

Breathe steady. Stay calm. Look for an escape.

The latch clicked on a door somewhere behind him. Every muscle tensed involuntarily. He breathed deeply to calm his nerves.

A drop of sweat raced from his right temple to his jaw.

Stay calm.

About The Author

Lisa Pietsch (pen name of Lisa Woodward) is the Publishing Director at Defiance Press and Publishing, an Air Force Veteran, former magazine publisher, multi-published author, mother of two giants, and wife to a Viking.

Lisa speaks French, Spanish, Norwegian, and Russian. She has been USAF Security Forces Leader, received specialized training as an FBI Hostage Negotiator, and worked with MI-5 on personal security details for both British and Jordanian Royals. These diverse experiences inspire her Task Force 125 series, which follows Sarah Stevens, a CIA Special Activities Division recruit, through gripping tales of espionage and paramilitary operations.

In 2020, Lisa's life took a romantic turn when she reconnected with the love of her life, the man who inspired her Task Force 125 series, launching her into her greatest adventure yet.

An avid gamer, Lisa enjoys both console and tabletop gaming, where she goes by "Geniekin" on Xbox and Roll20.

As Lisa Pietsch, she crafts thrilling paramilitary action/adventure/romance novels, while as Lisa Woodward, she weaves enchanting epic romantic fantasy tales.